Sports Illustrated KIDS
GRAPHIC NOVELS

STONE ARCH BOOKS
a capstone imprint

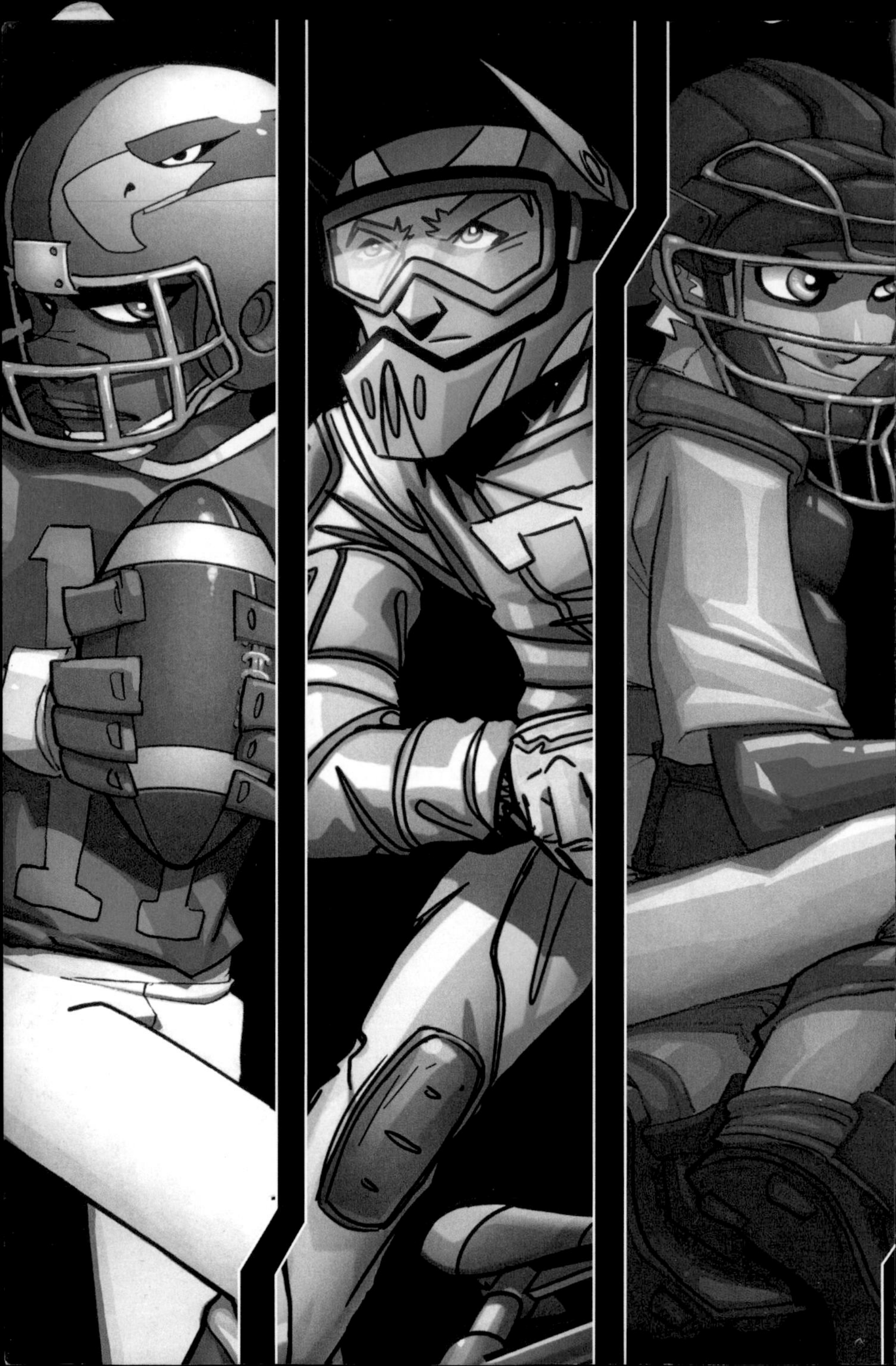

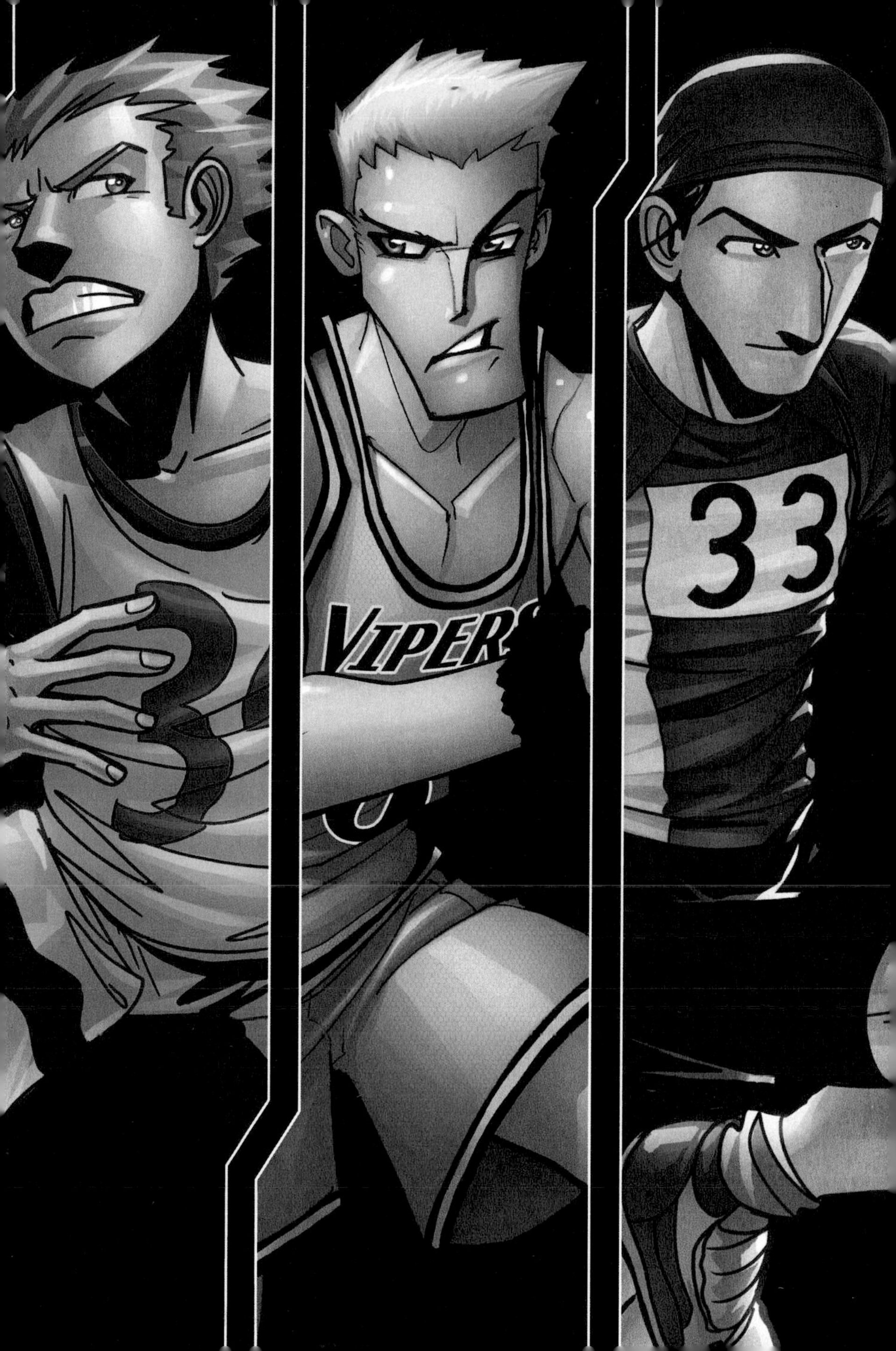
VIPERS
33

UP NEXT ›››

on Sports Illustrated KIDS

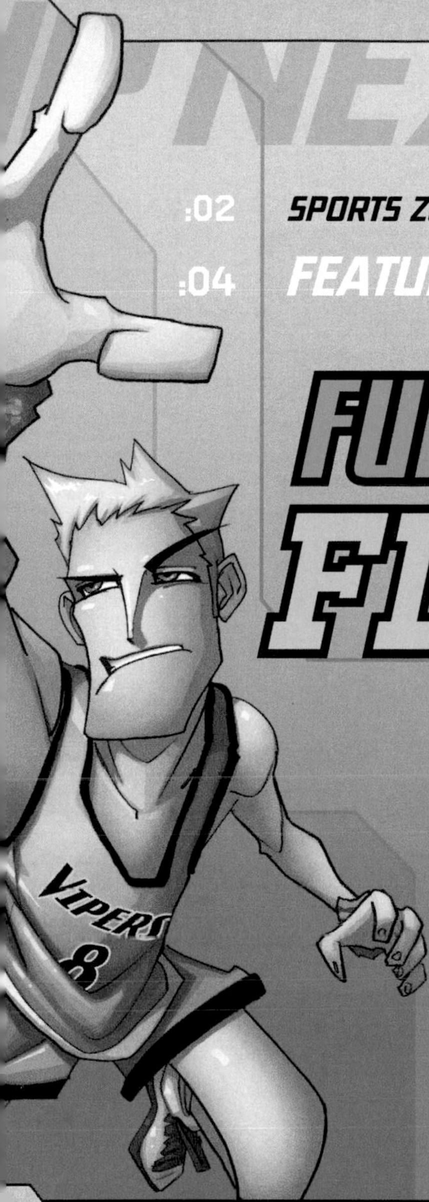
VIPERS
8

:02 SPORTS ZONE SPECIAL REPORT

:04 FEATURE PRESENTATION:

FULL COURT FLASH

FOLLOWED BY:

:50 SPORTS ZONE POSTGAME RECAP

:51 SPORTS ZONE POSTGAME EXTRA

:52 SI KIDS INFO CENTER

DASH THE FLASH LEADS LEAGUE IN REBOUNDS, POINTS, ASSIS SIK TICKER

SPORTS ZONE
SPECIAL REPORT

BBL
BASKETBALL

PNT
PAINTBALL

FBL
FOOTBALL

BSL
BASEBALL

BBL
BASKETBALL

UNSTOPPABLE FORCE MEETS IMMOVABLE OBJECT

DASH THE FLASH

STATS:
AGE: 14
TEAM: VIPERS

BIO: Dash the Flash, named for his impressive offensive arsenal, has been running wild on the opposition all season. As Dash sees it, he's unstoppable, and few of his opponents would disagree with him — except one: Jay the Juggernaut. Jay is so named for his ability to decide the outcome of any game he's in. If Dash the Flash can be stopped, Jay the Juggernaut is the one to do it.

Sports Illustrated KIDS

UP NEXT: FULL COURT FLASH

JAY THE JUGGERNAUT

AGE: 15
TEAM: GOLIATHS
BIO: If Dash is an unstoppable force, Jay is an immovable object. Getting around Jay is next to impossible — he has crab-like lateral movement capabilities, and he anticipates his opponents' moves quite easily, making him the toughest competition Dash has yet to see.

BLZ vs BMS
3-1
TGR vs ROR
33-32
EAG vs BAN
14-7
SPA vs WLO
4-3
BAN vs ROR
21-15
RZR vs LIG
4-3
BLZ vs BMS
3-1

DAN

AGE: 14 **TEAM:** GOLIATHS
BIO: Dan is the Goliaths' team captain. He tries to keep Jay on a tight leash, but Jay tends to do whatever he wants.

DAN

ANDY

AGE: 14 **TEAM:** VIPERS
BIO: Andy has the best hands on the Vipers. He always comes through when it counts and has a positive outlook that rallies his teammates.

ANDY

JULIO

AGE: 14 **TEAM:** VIPERS
BIO: Julio doesn't get passed to very often. He's very quiet — no one quite knows what to make of the kid.

JULIO

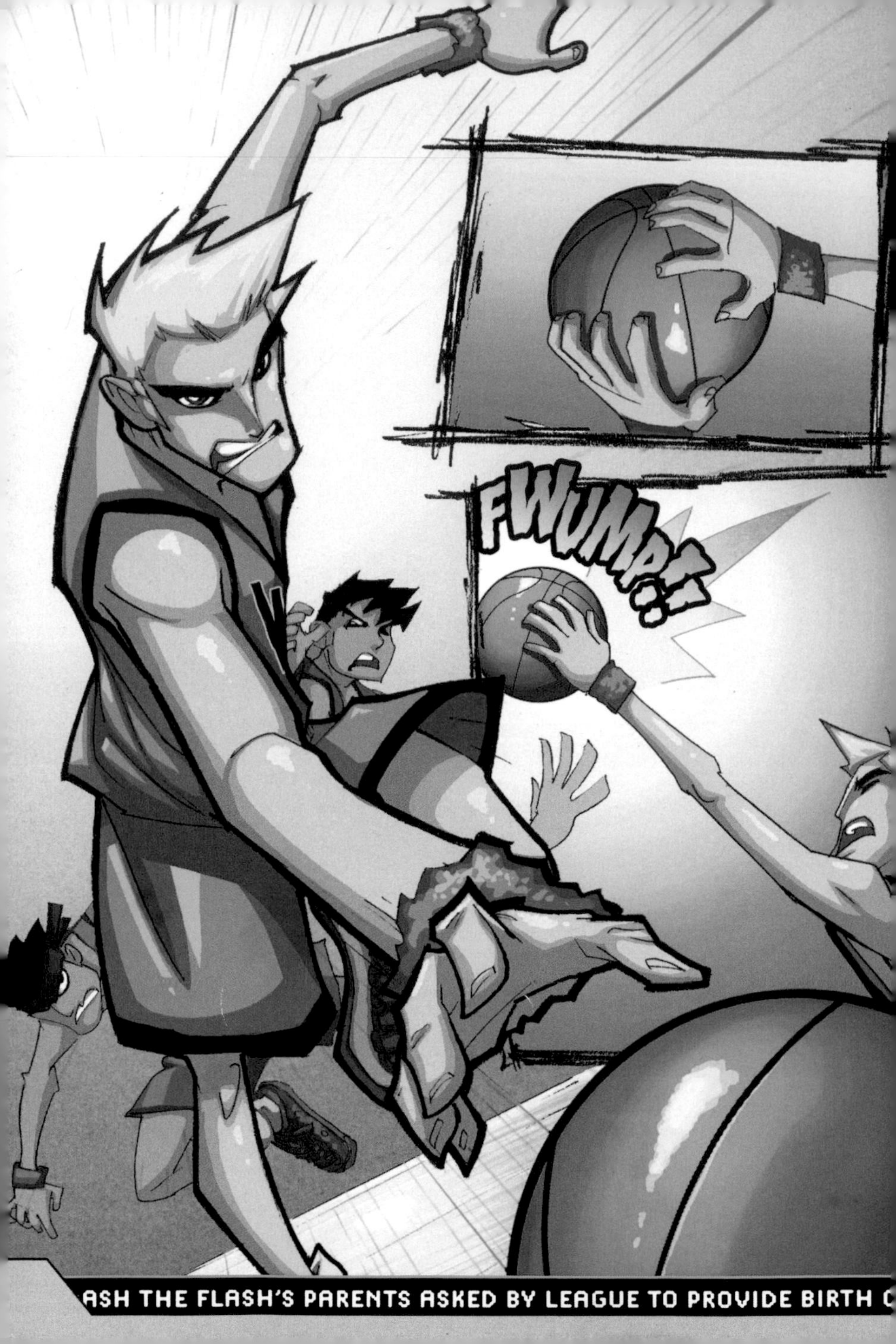
FWUMP!!
ASH THE FLASH'S PARENTS ASKED BY LEAGUE TO PROVIDE BIRTH C

Sports Illustrated KIDS

PRESENTS

FULL COURT FLASH

A PRODUCTION OF

STONE ARCH BOOKS
a capstone imprint

written by Scott Ciencin
illustrated by Gerardo Sandoval
colored by Benny Fuentes

designed and directed by Bob Lentz
edited by Sean Tulien
creative direction by Heather Kindseth
editorial management by Donald Lemke
editorial direction by Michael Dahl

Sports Illustrated KIDS *Full Court Flash* is published by Stone Arch Books,
1710 Roe Crest Drive, North Mankato, Minnesota 56003.
www.capstonepub.com

Printed in the United States of America.
061920 003607

Summary: Dash the Flash grew nearly a foot last year. Now, he's taller than everyone else. Dash out jumps defenders and sinks big shots, all while making it look too easy. There's just one problem — his teammates can't keep up! His passes are missing the mark, and his friends are getting frustrated with his one man show. Dash has some work to do to prove he's not all Flash and no substance.

Library of Congress Cataloging-in-Publication Data
Ciencin, Scott.
Full court flash / written by Scott Ciencin ; illustrated by Gerardo Sandoval and Benny Fuentes.
p. cm. -- (Sports Illustrated kids graphic novels)
ISBN 978-1-4342-2225-1 (library binding)
ISBN 978-1-4342-3074-4 (paperback)
ISBN 978-1-4342-4943-2 (e-book)
1. Graphic novels. [1. Graphic novels. 2. Basketball--Fiction. 3. Teamwork (Sports)--Fiction.] I. Sandoval, Gerardo ill. II. Fuentes, Benny, ill. III. Title.
PZ7.7.C54Fu 2011
741.5'973--dc22 2010032812

TE TO PROVE THAT THE TALENTED TEEN IS ONLY 14 YEARS (SIK TICKER

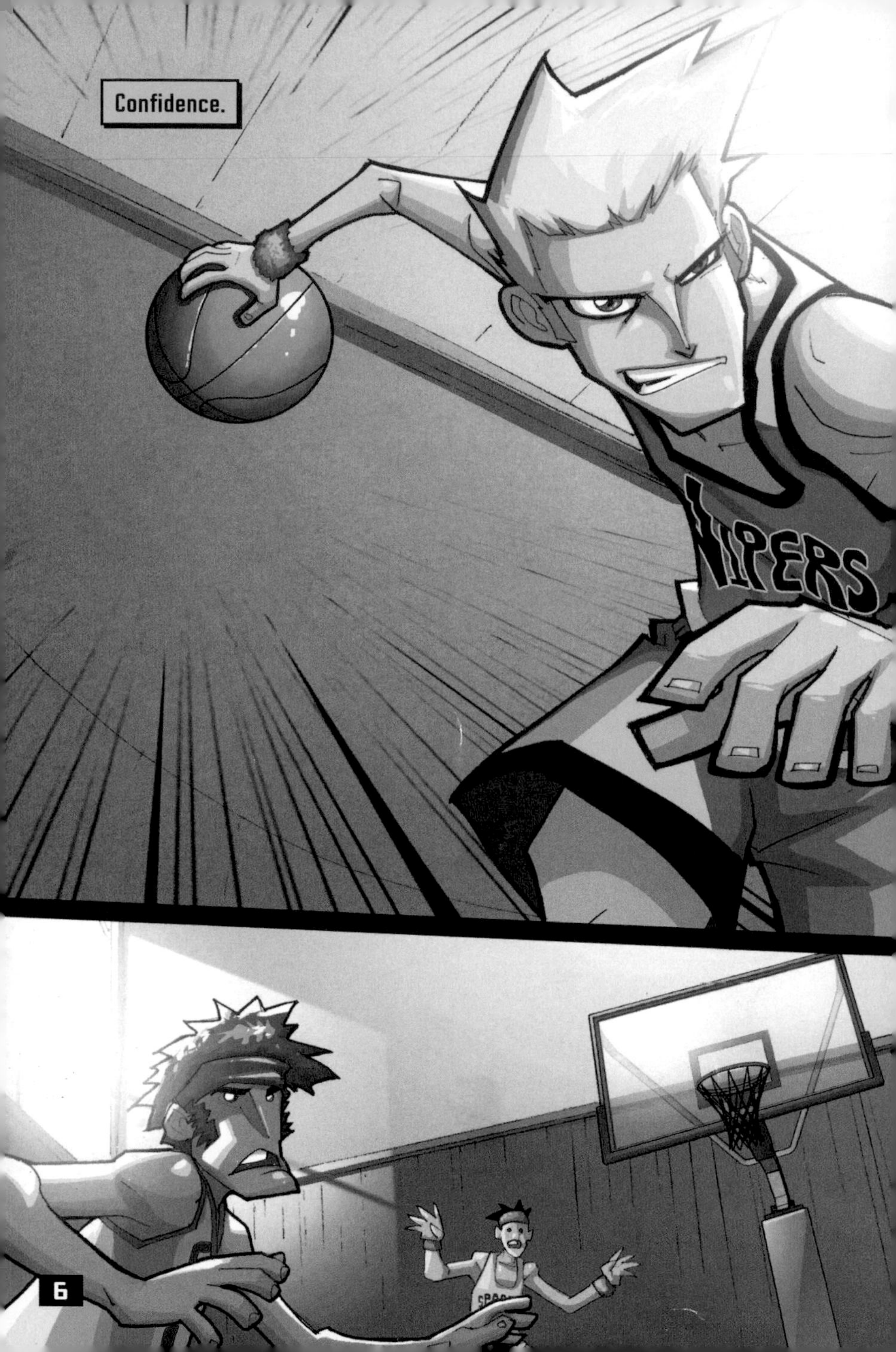
Confidence.

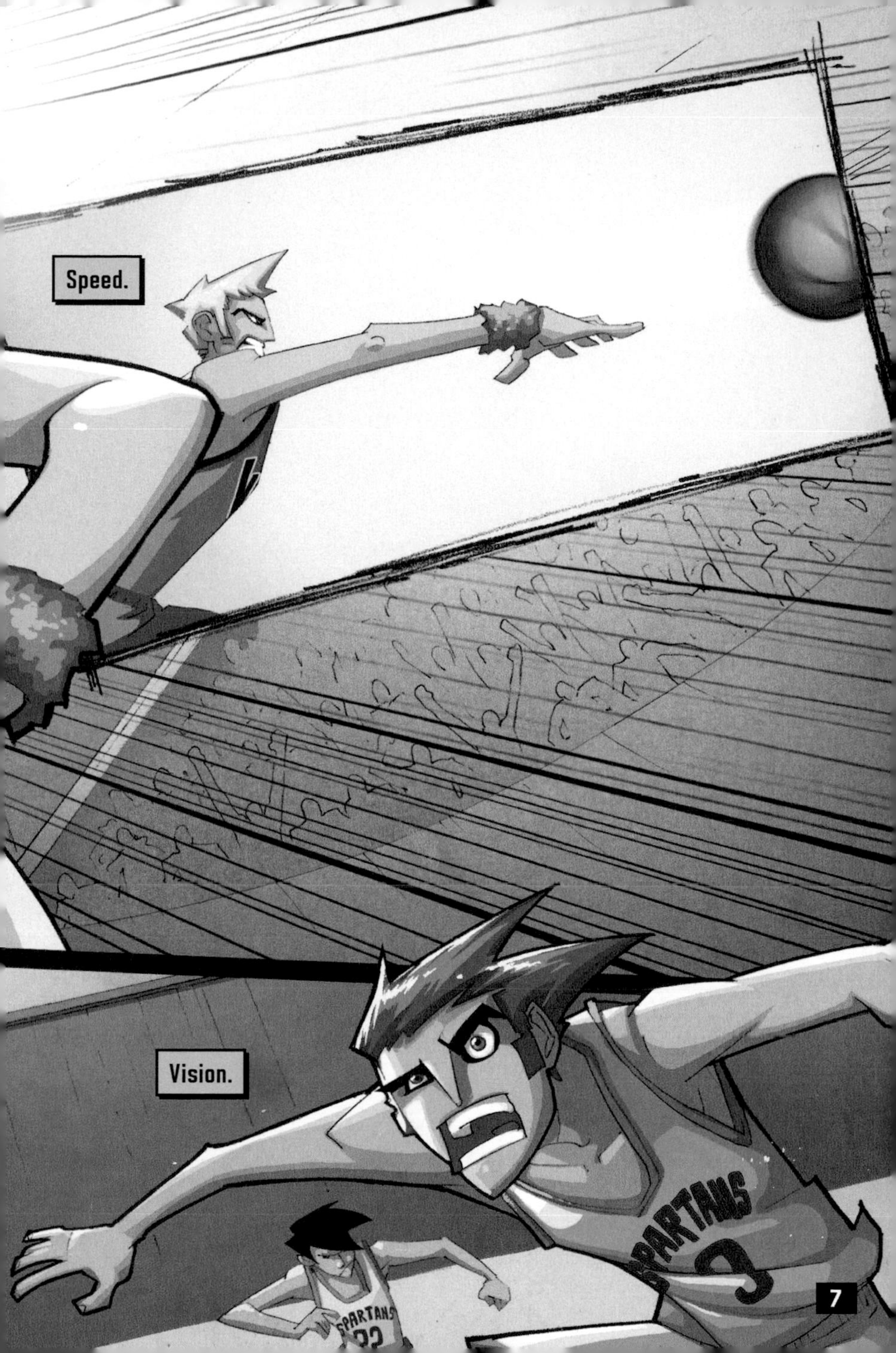
Speed.
Vision.
SPARTANS
3
SPARTANS
22

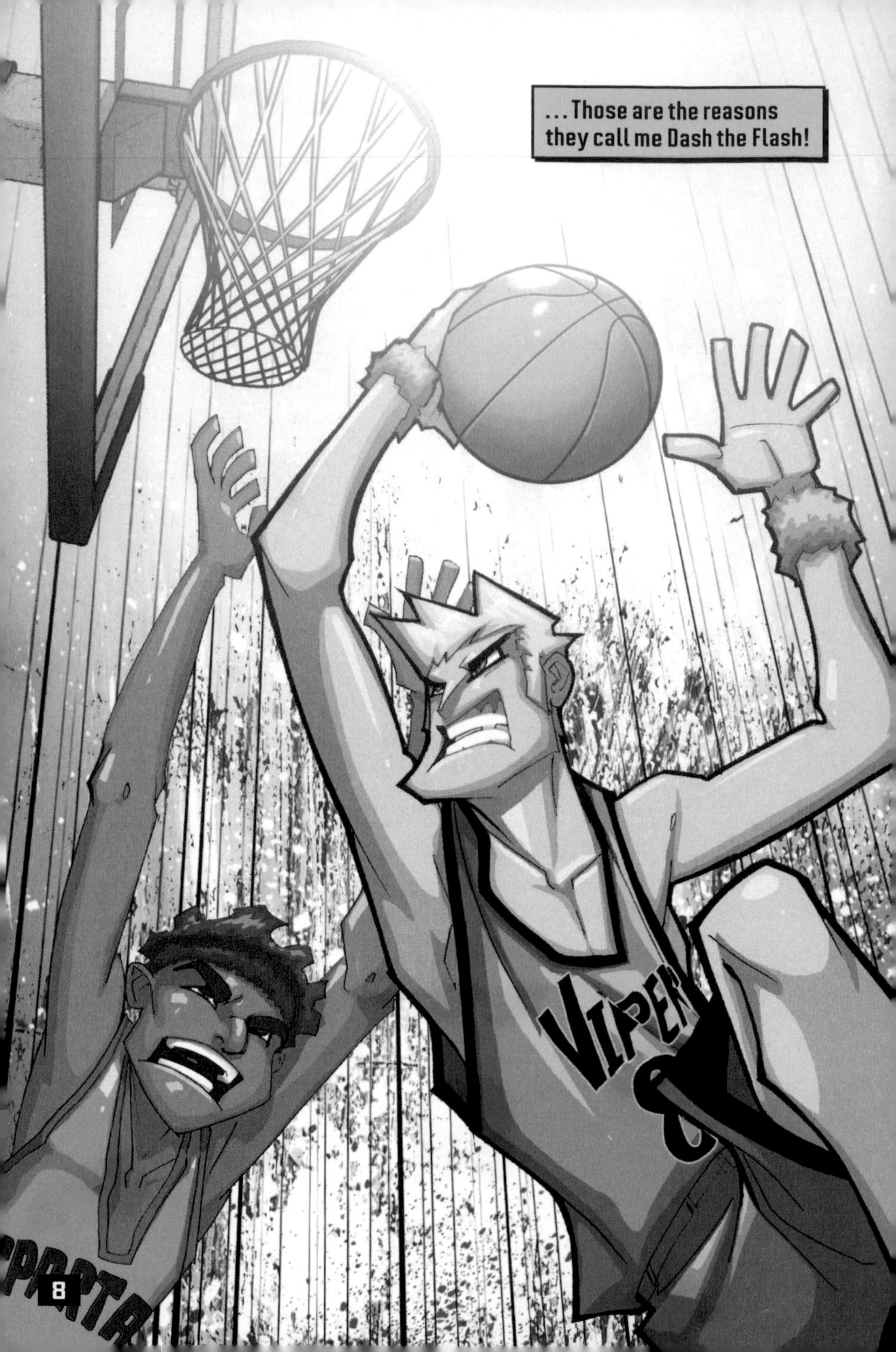
...Those are the reasons they call me Dash the Flash!
VIPER
SPARTA

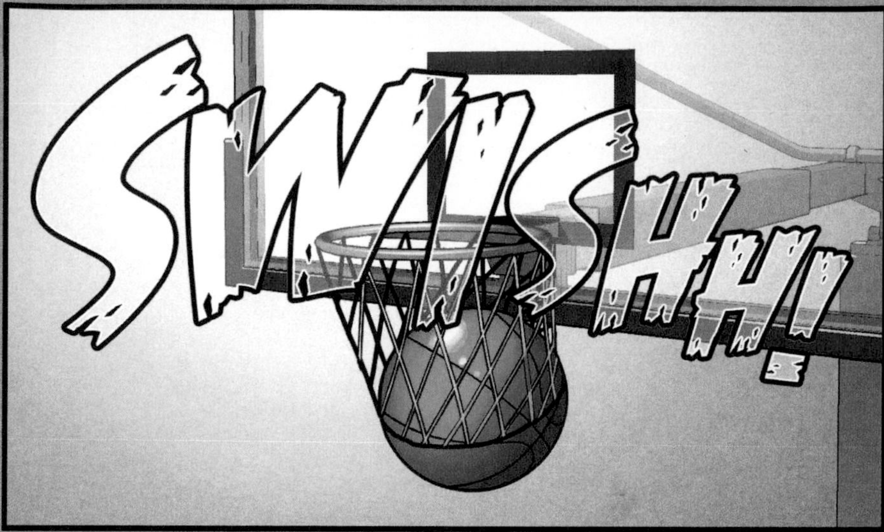
SWISHH!

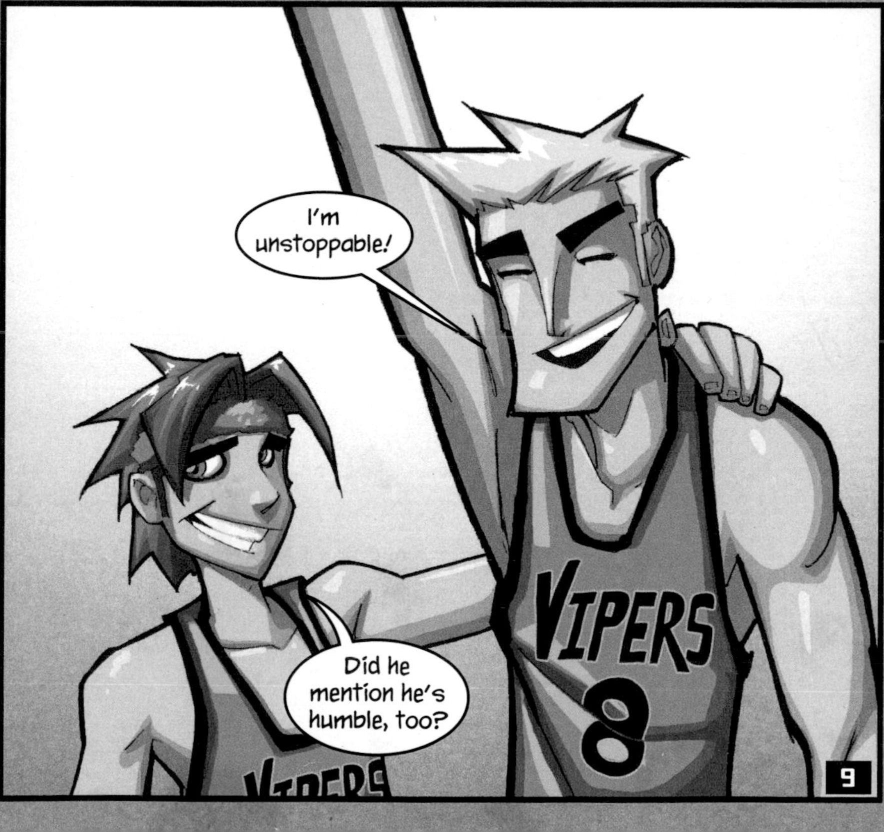
I'm unstoppable!
Did he mention he's humble, too?
VIPERS
8

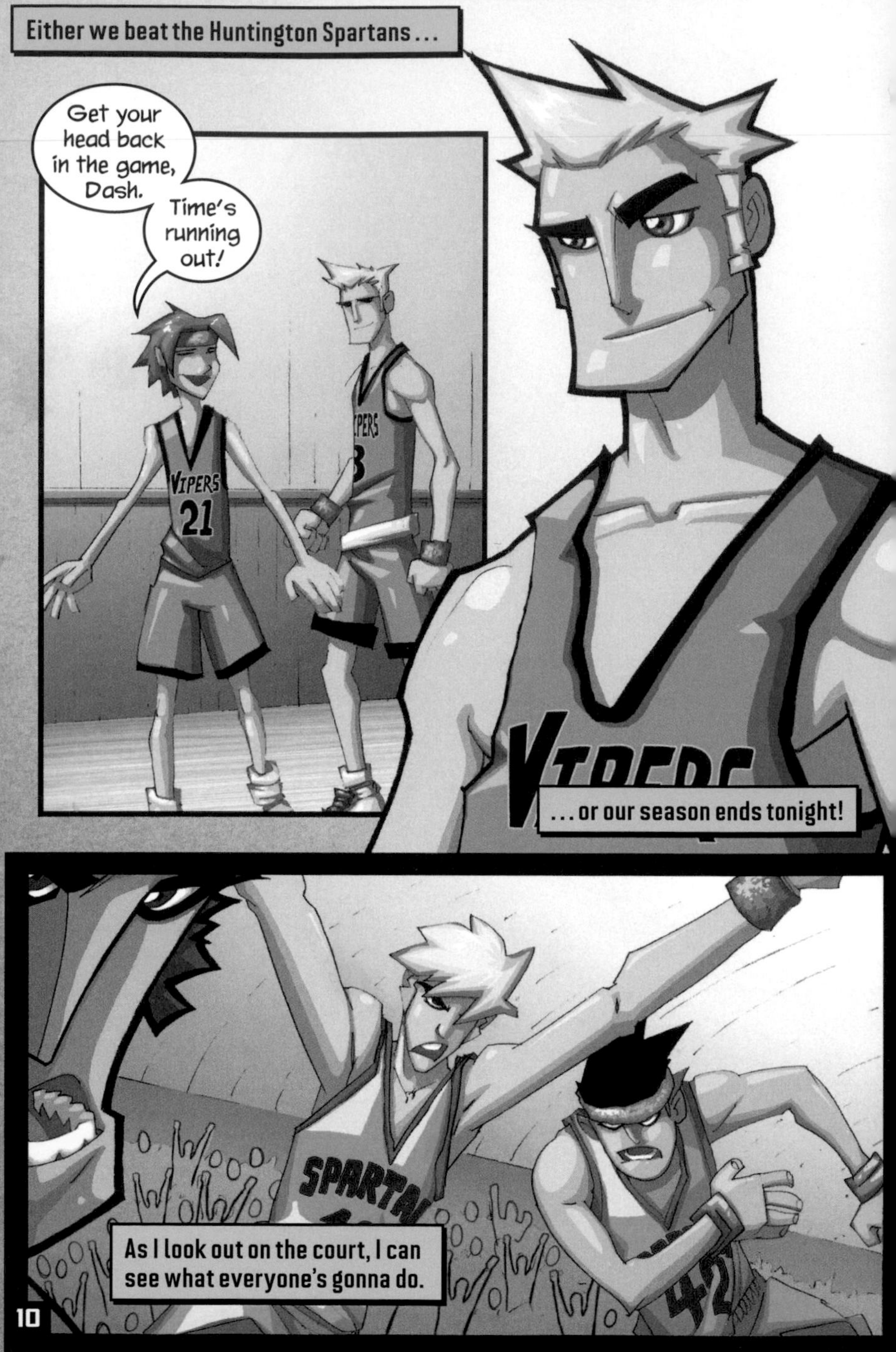
Either we beat the Huntington Spartans . . .
Get your head back in the game, Dash.
Time's running out!
VIPERS
21
. . . or our season ends tonight!
SPARTA
42
As I look out on the court, I can see what everyone's gonna do.

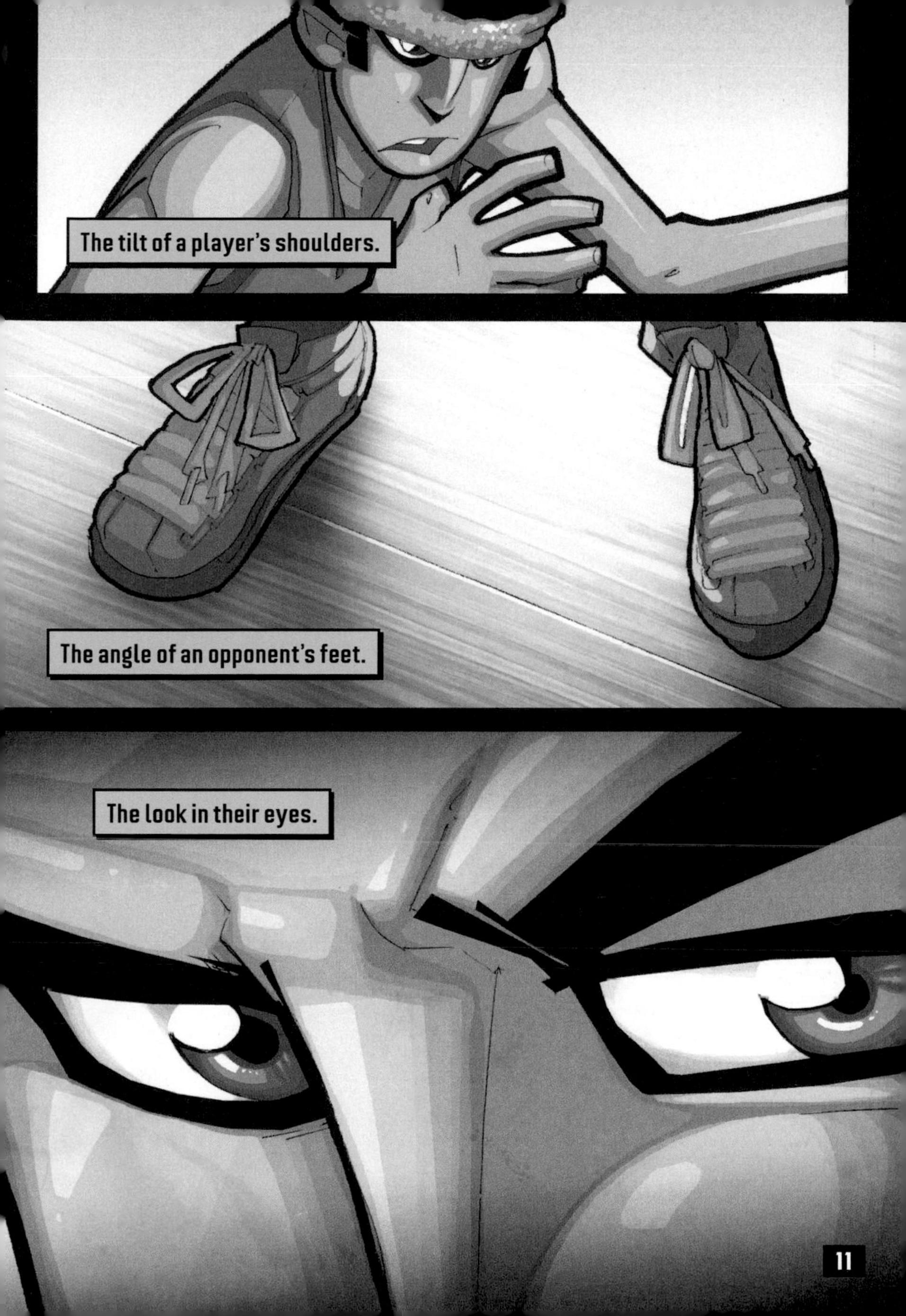
The tilt of a player's shoulders.
The angle of an opponent's feet.
The look in their eyes.

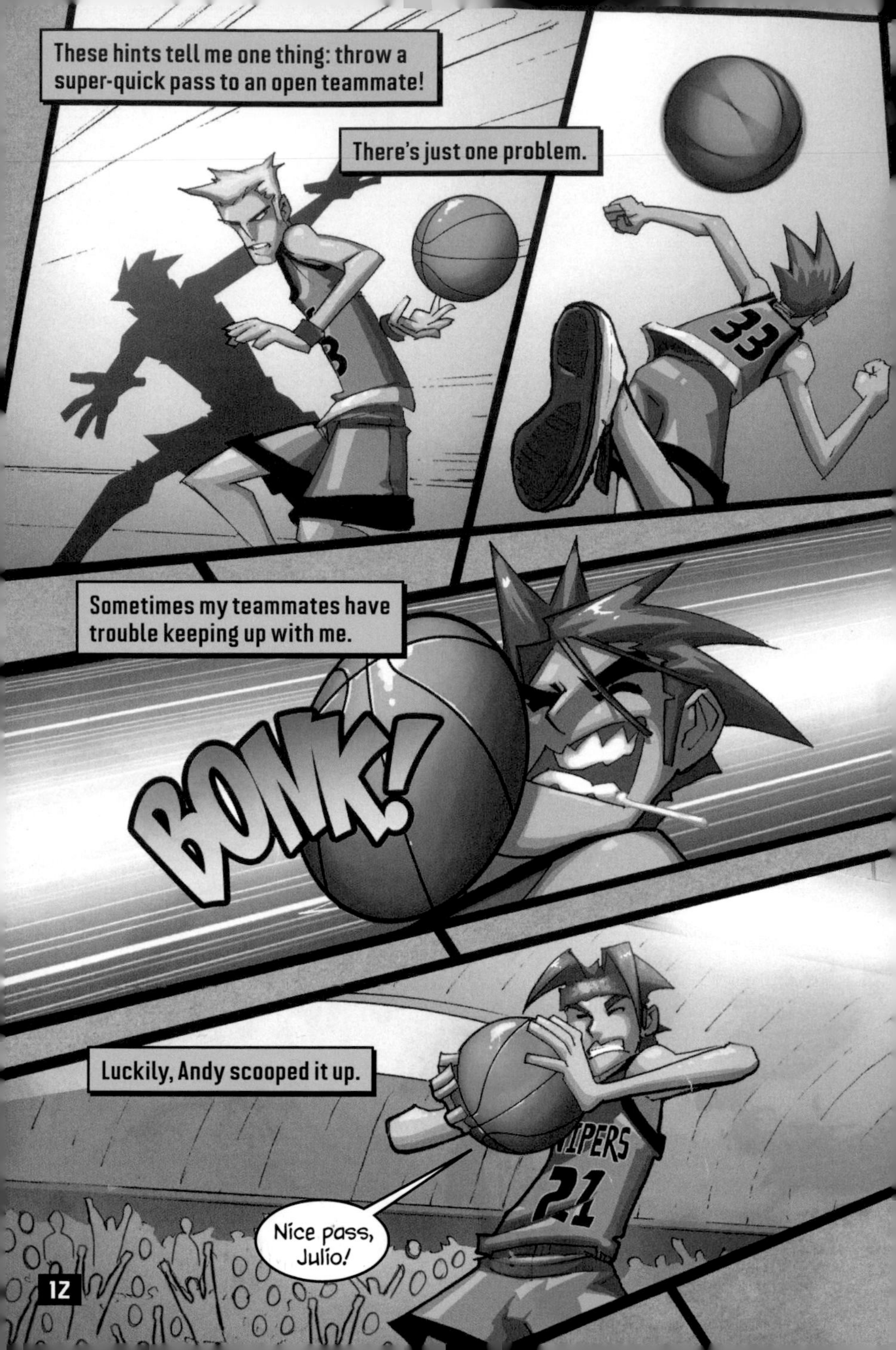
These hints tell me one thing: throw a super-quick pass to an open teammate!
There's just one problem.
33
Sometimes my teammates have trouble keeping up with me.
BONK!
Luckily, Andy scooped it up.
VIPERS
21
Nice pass, Julio!

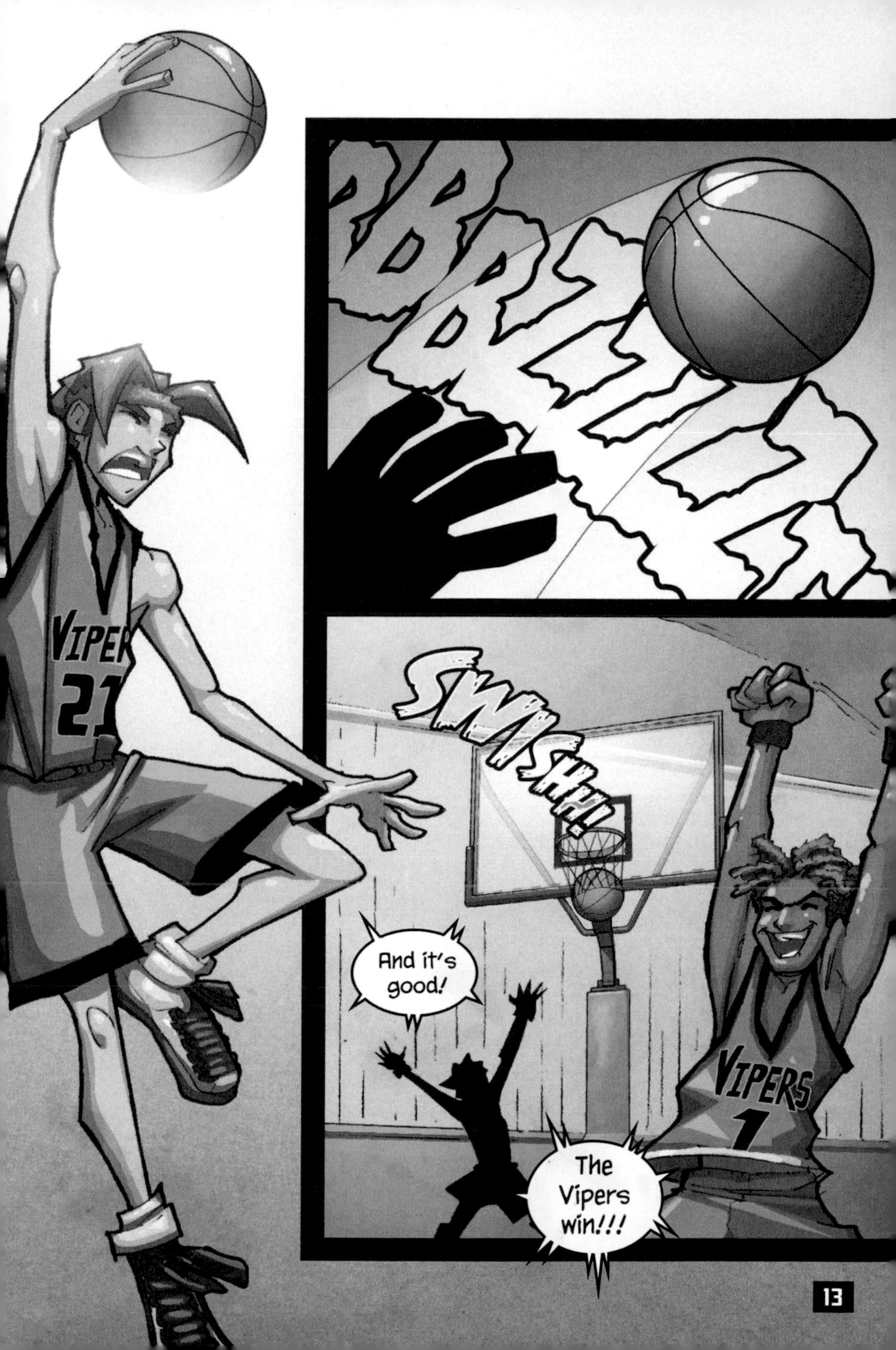
VIPERS
21
BRZZZZT
SWISH!
And it's good!
VIPERS
1
The Vipers win!!!

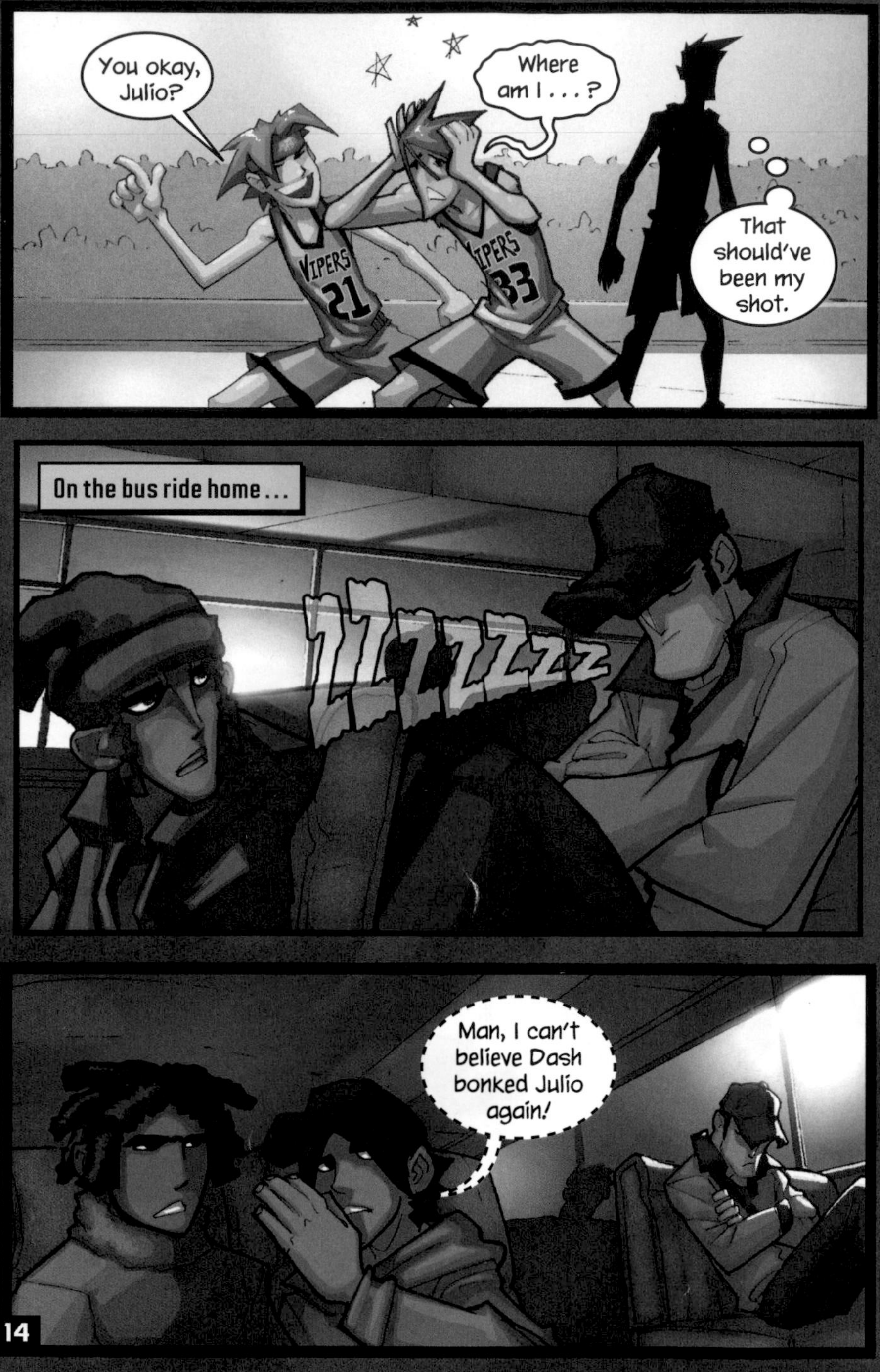
You okay, Julio?
Where am I . . . ?
VIPERS 21
VIPERS 33
That should've been my shot.
On the bus ride home . . .
ZZZZZzzz
Man, I can't believe Dash bonked Julio again!

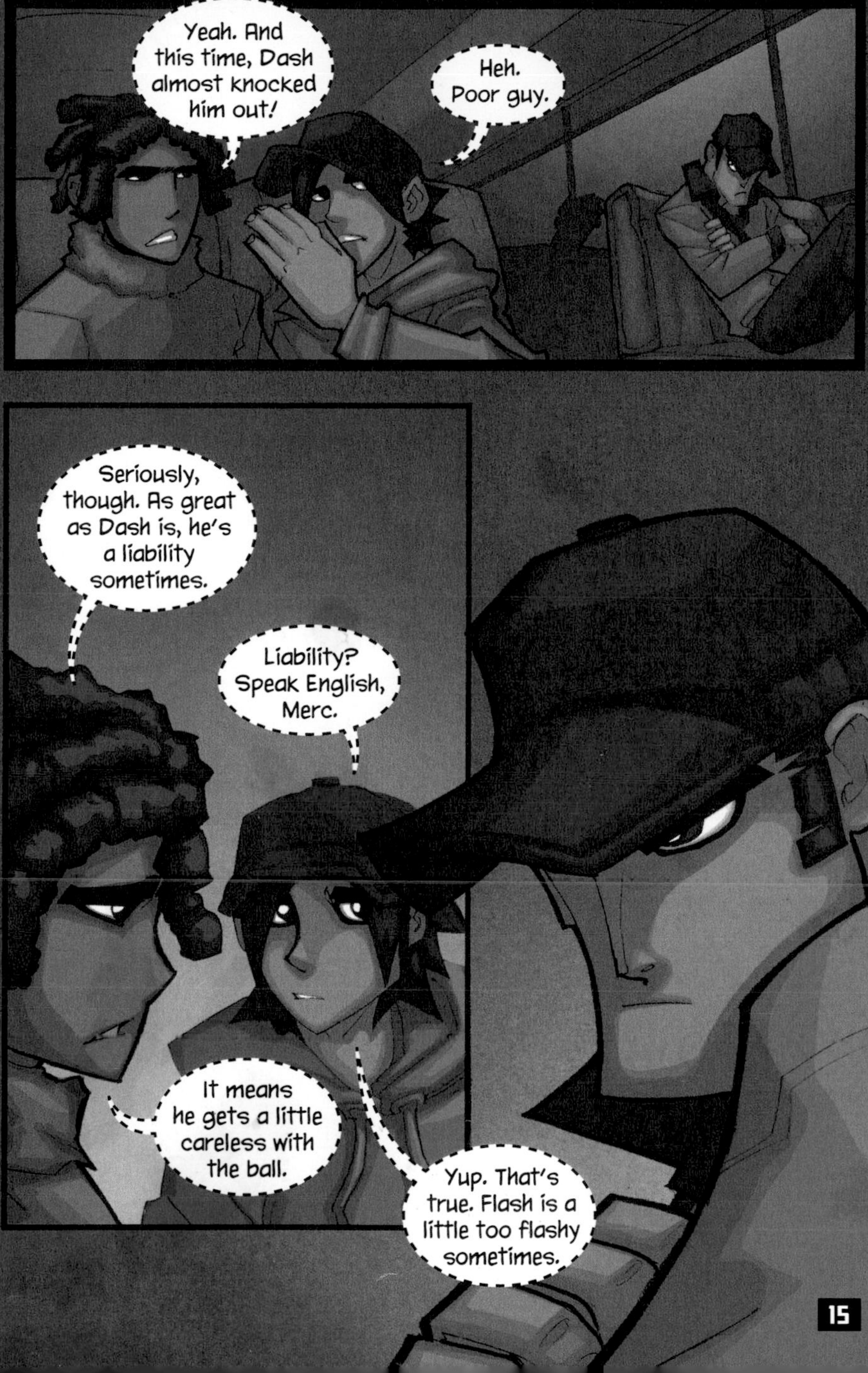
Yeah. And this time, Dash almost knocked him out!
Heh. Poor guy.
Seriously, though. As great as Dash is, he's a liability sometimes.
Liability? Speak English, Merc.
It means he gets a little careless with the ball.
Yup. That's true. Flash is a little too flashy sometimes.

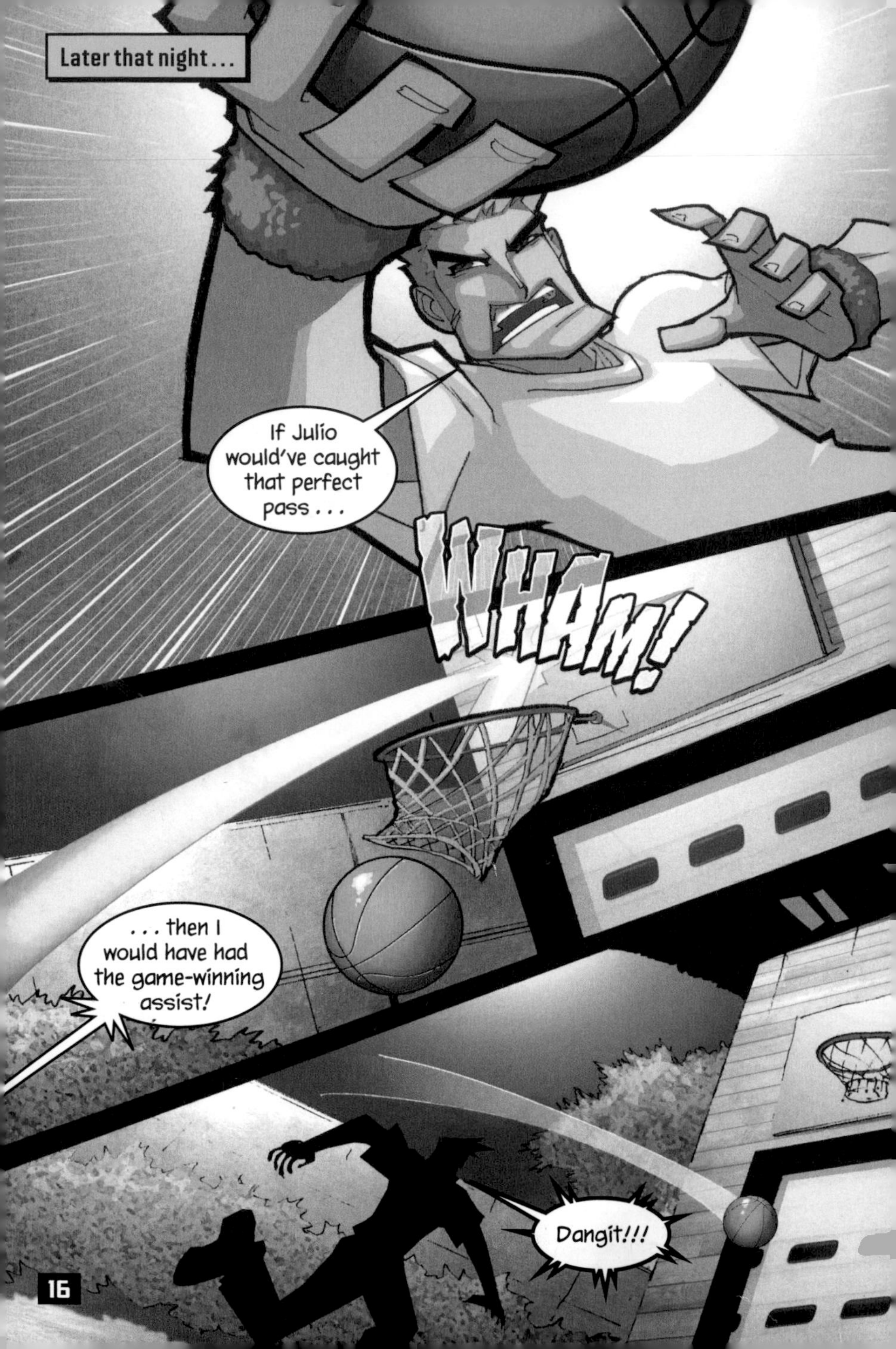

Later that night . . .
If Julio would've caught that perfect pass . . .
WHAM!
. . . then I would have had the game-winning assist!
Dangit!!!

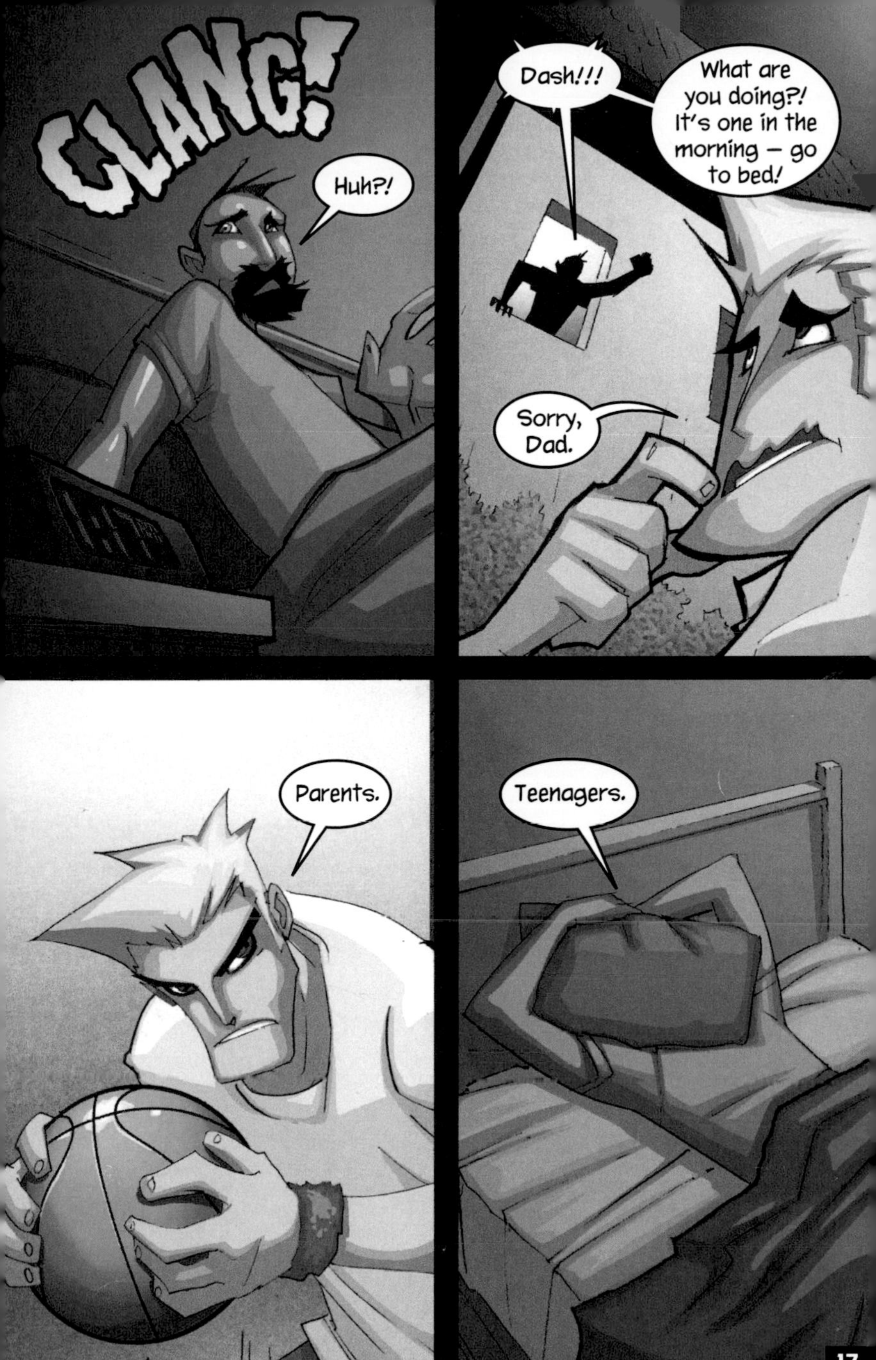
CLANG!
Huh?!
Dash!!!
What are you doing?! It's one in the morning – go to bed!
Sorry, Dad.
Parents.
Teenagers.

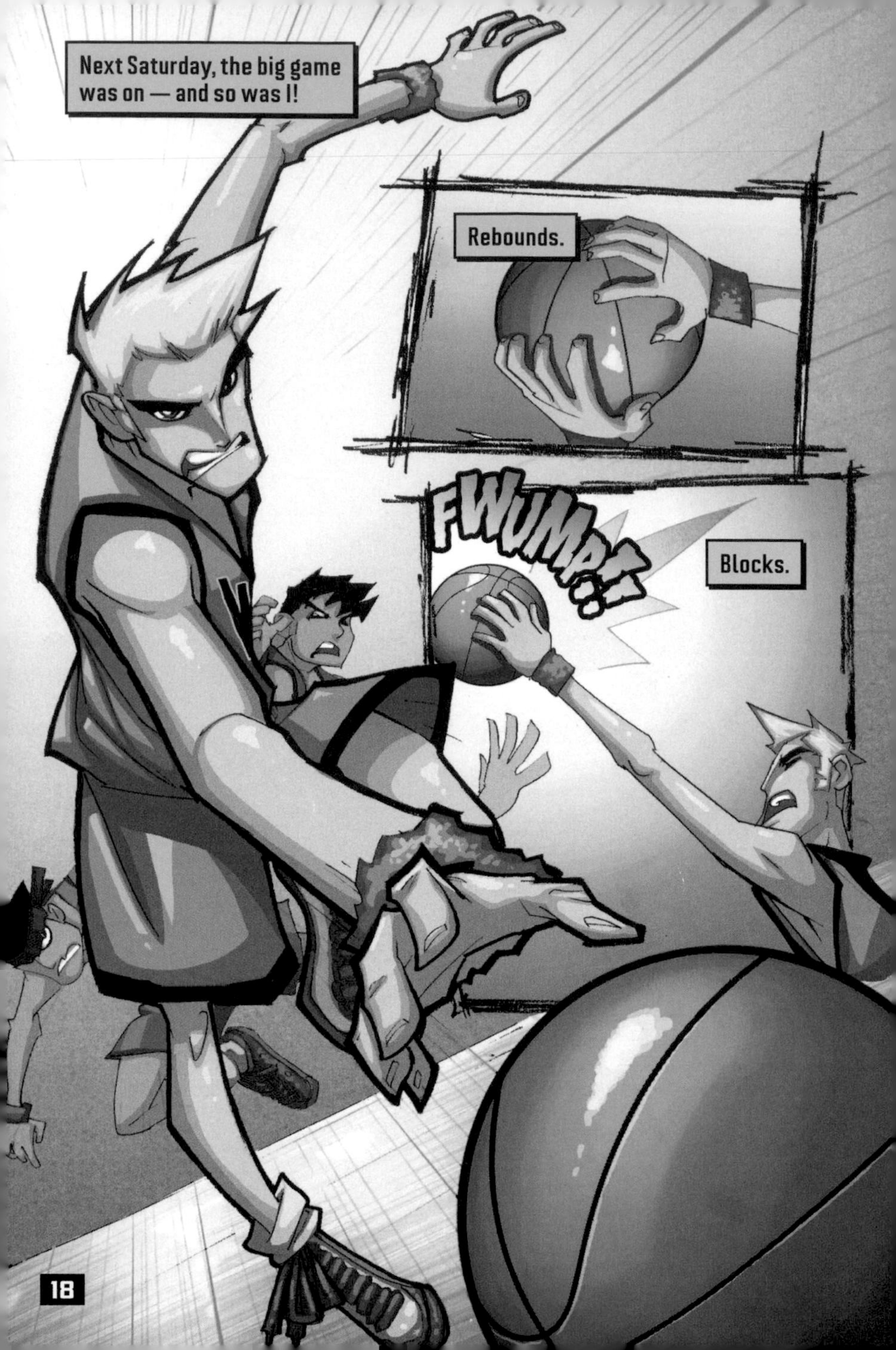
Next Saturday, the big game was on — and so was I!
Rebounds.
FWUMP!!
Blocks.

Steals.

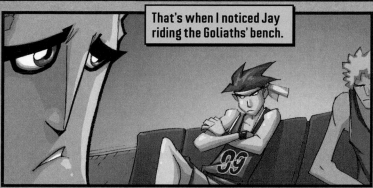

That's when I noticed Jay riding the Goliaths' bench.

Rumor is, he's been suspended because of his poor attitude.

It's too bad — I wanted to see who is better.

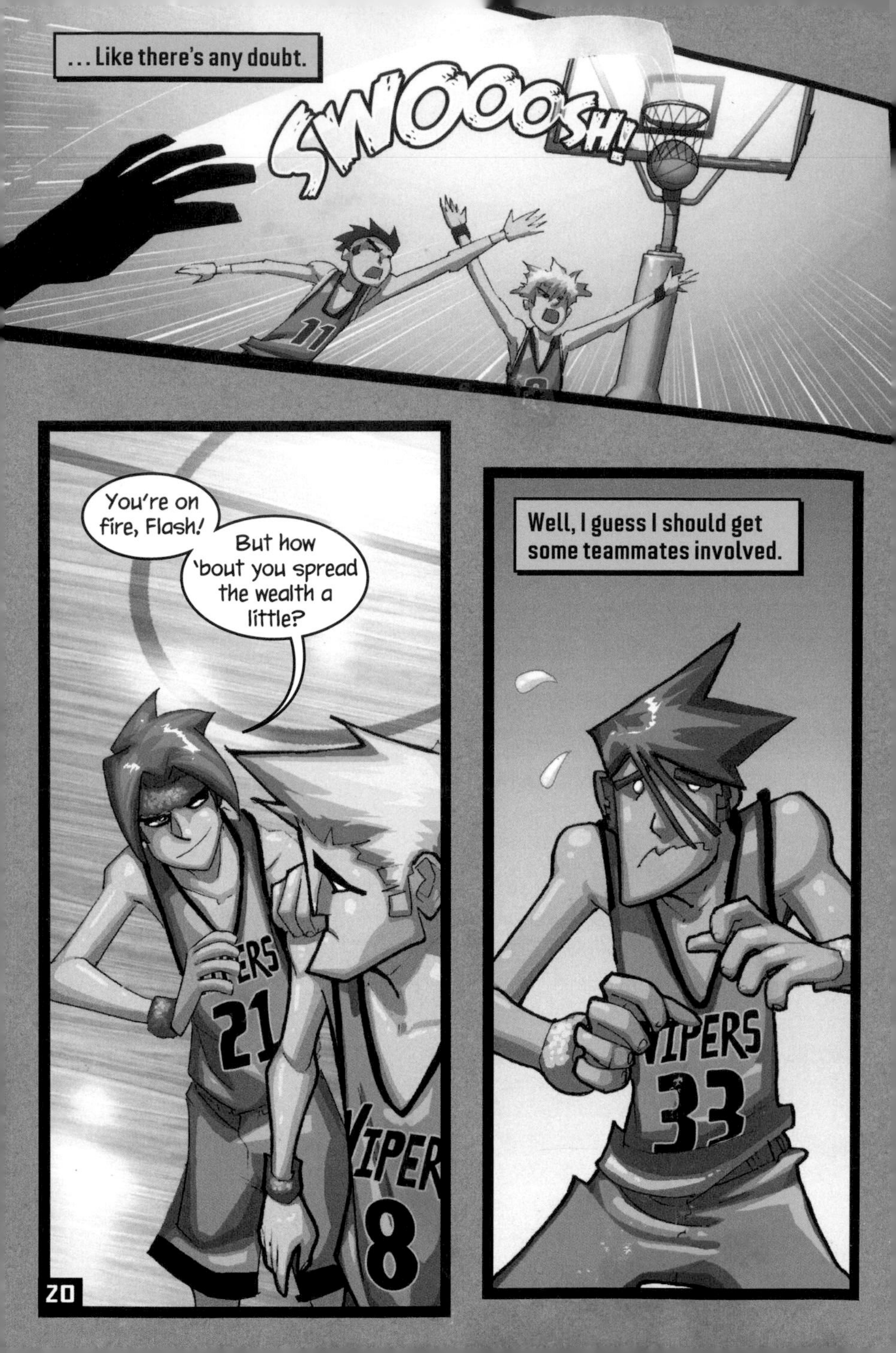
. . . Like there's any doubt.
SWOOOSH!
You're on fire, Flash!
But how 'bout you spread the wealth a little?
VIPERS 21
VIPERS 8
Well, I guess I should get some teammates involved.
VIPERS 33

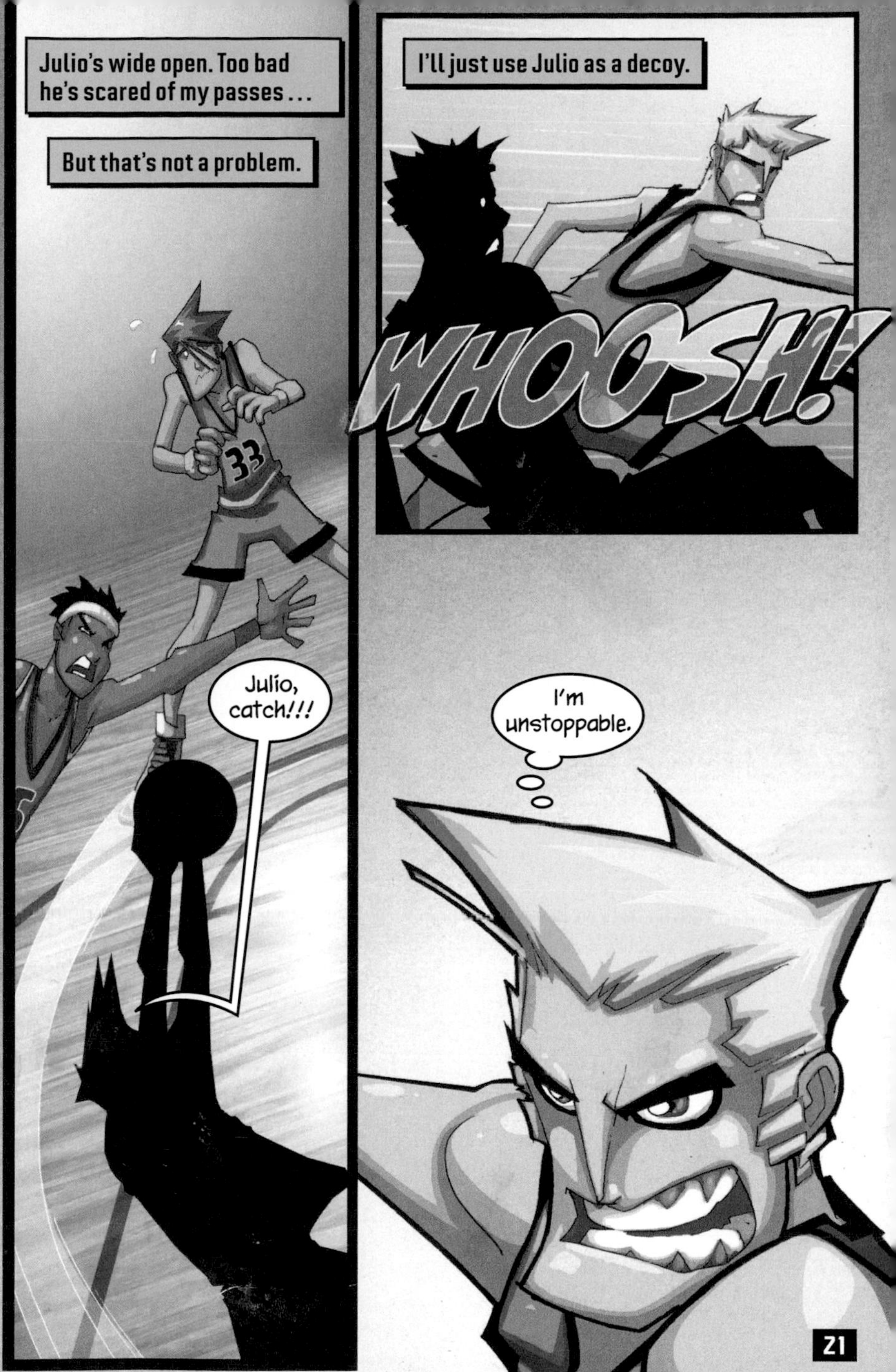

Julio's wide open. Too bad he's scared of my passes . . .
But that's not a problem.
Julio, catch!!!
I'll just use Julio as a decoy.
WHOOSH!
I'm unstoppable.

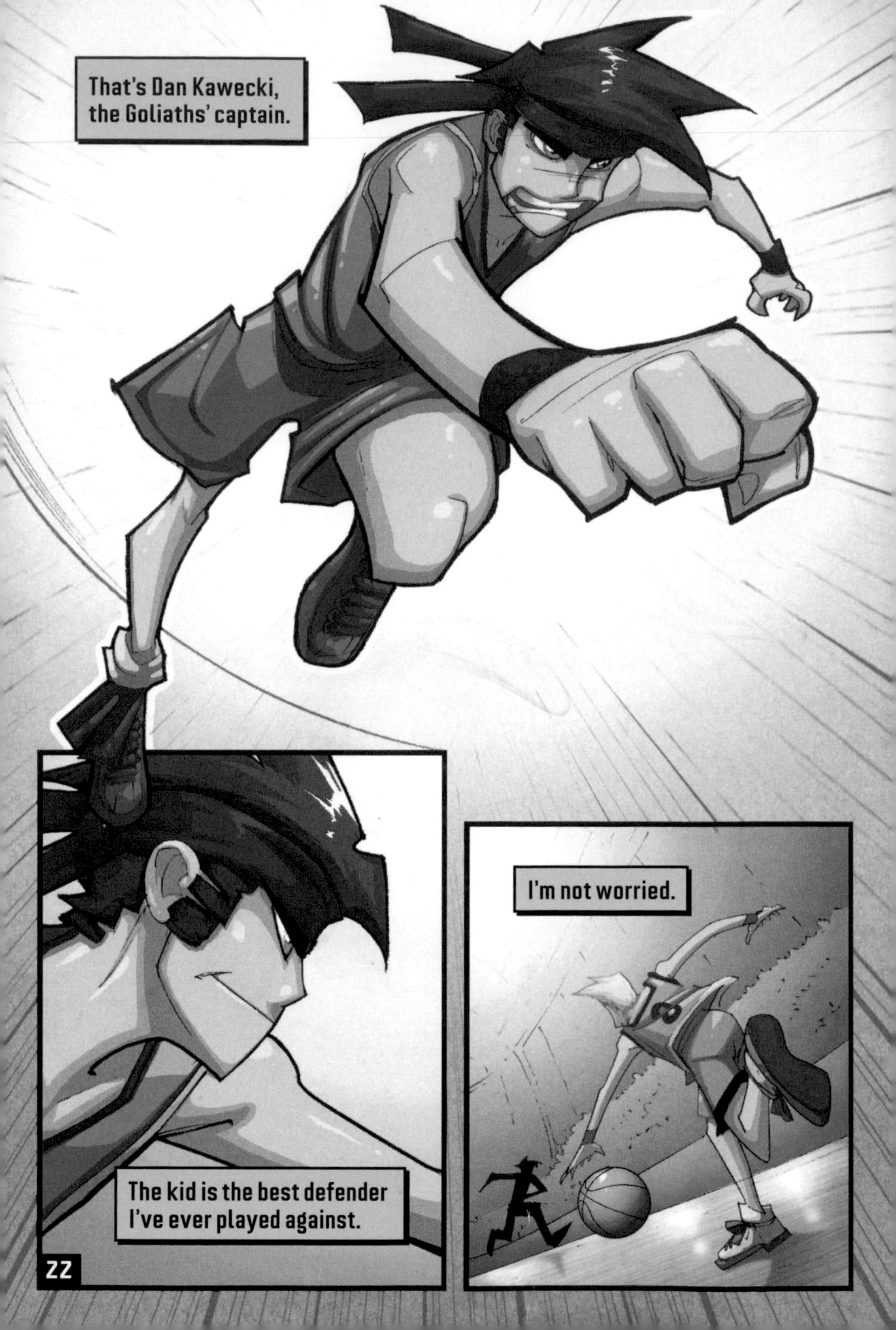
That's Dan Kawecki, the Goliaths' captain.
The kid is the best defender I've ever played against.
I'm not worried.

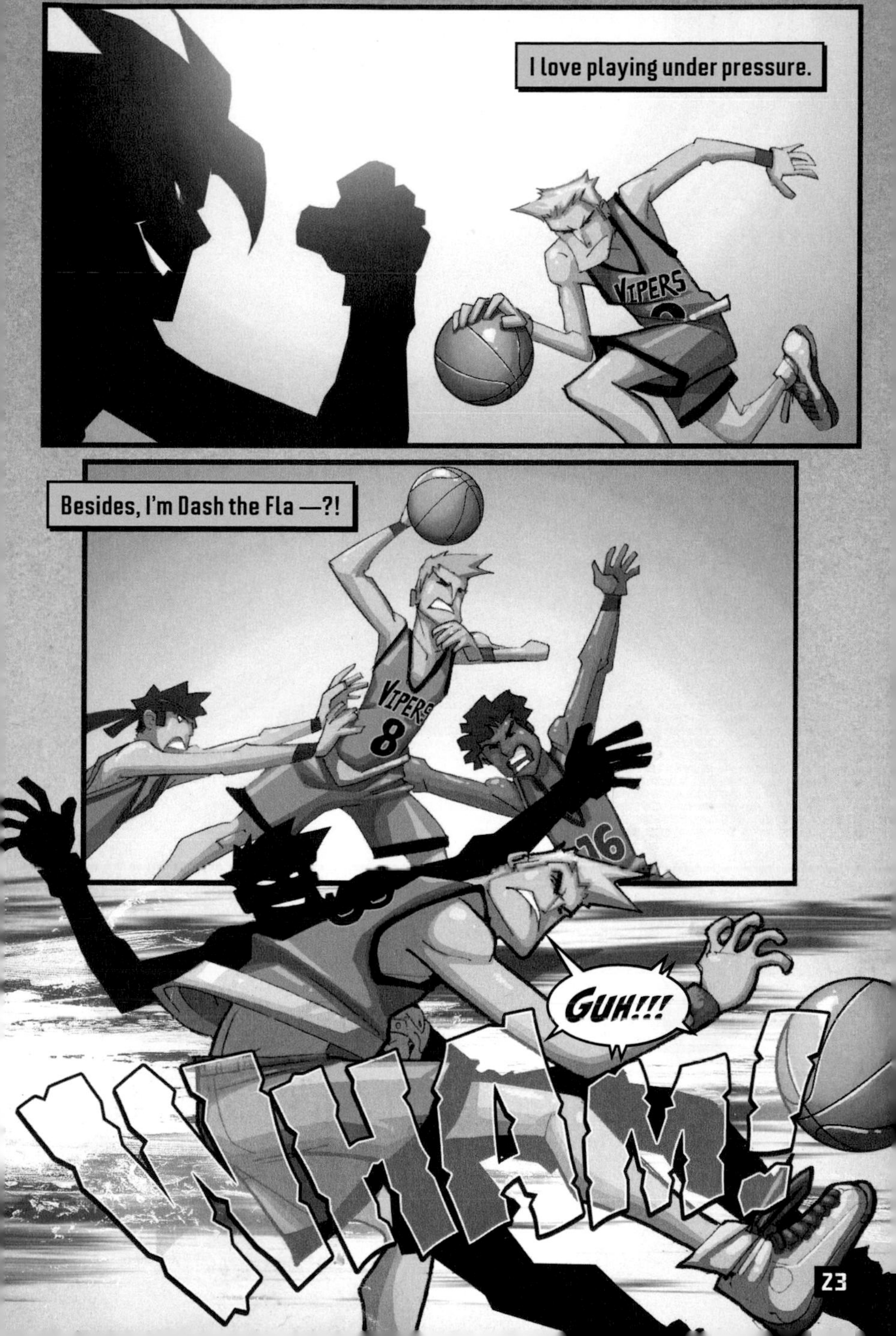
I love playing under pressure.
VIPERS
Besides, I'm Dash the Fla —?!
VIPERS
8
16
GUH!!!
WHAM!

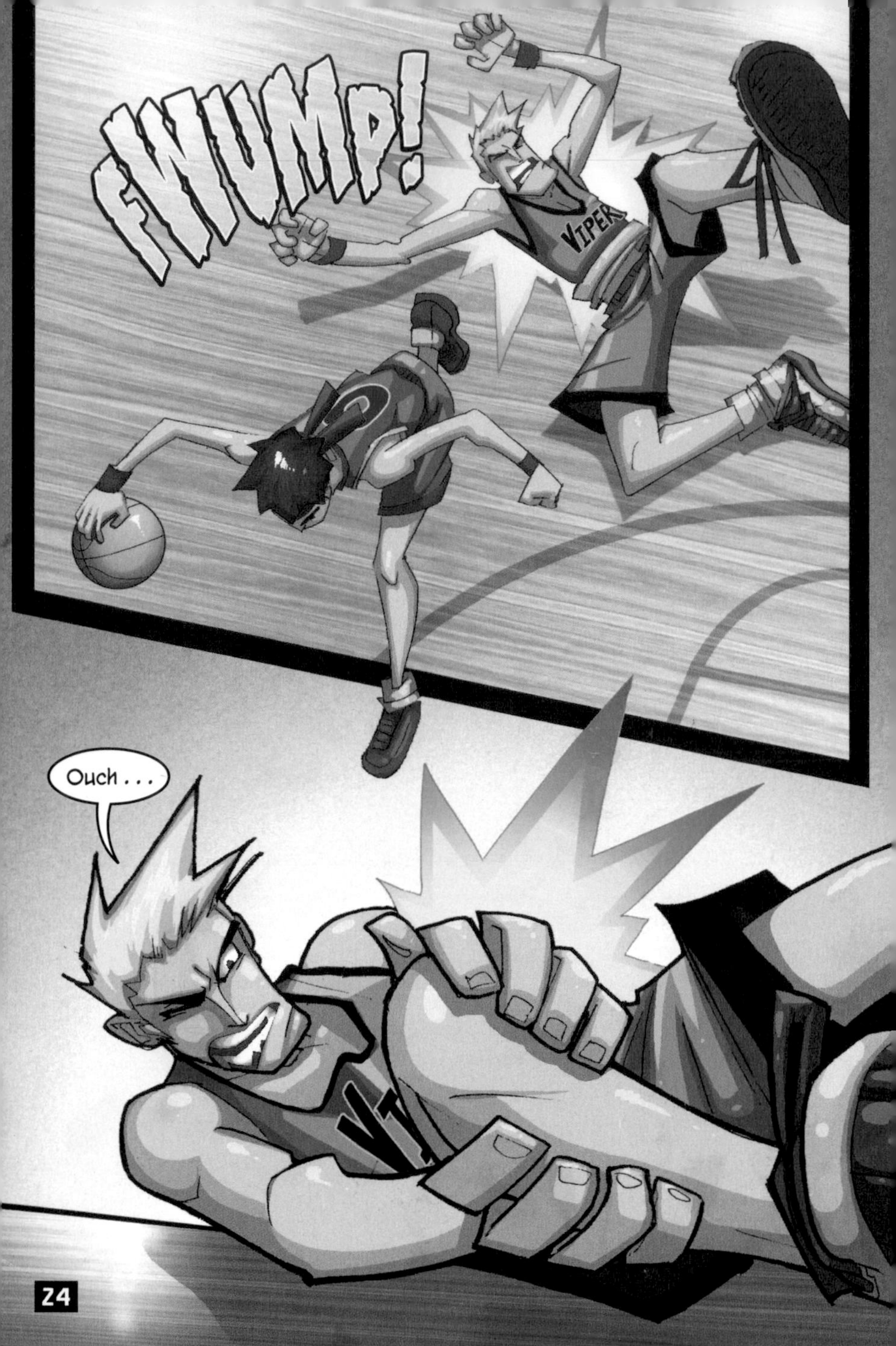
FWUMP!
VIPER
Ouch . . .

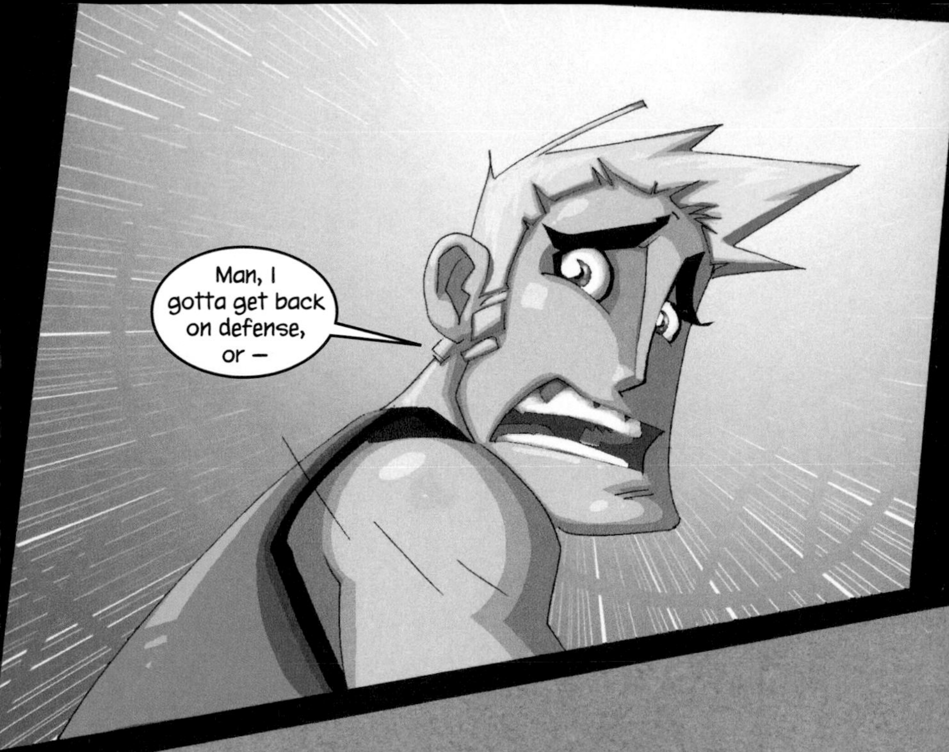
Man, I gotta get back on defense, or –

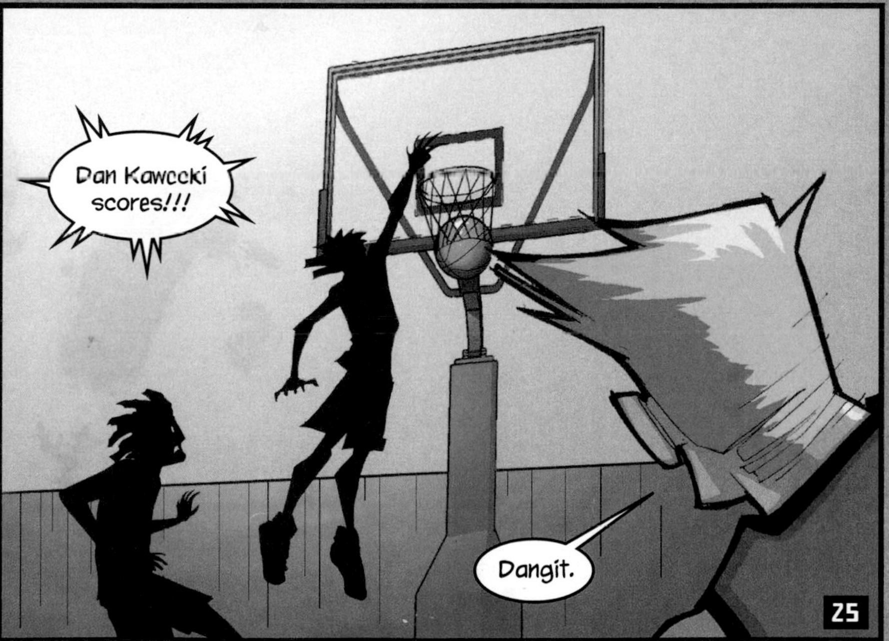
Dan Kawecki scores!!!
Dangit.

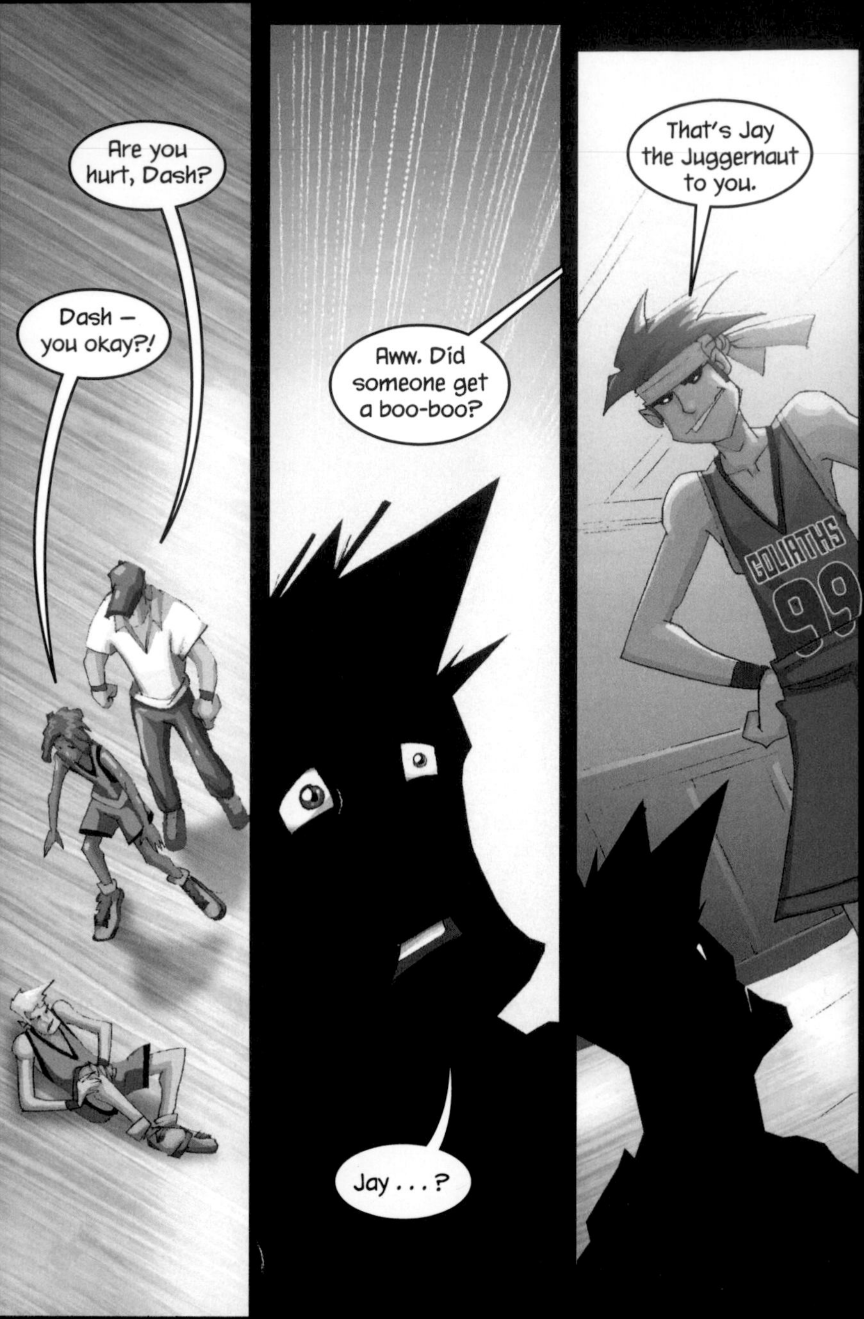
Dash — you okay?!
Are you hurt, Dash?
Aww. Did someone get a boo-boo?
Jay . . . ?
That's Jay the Juggernaut to you.
GOLIATHS
99

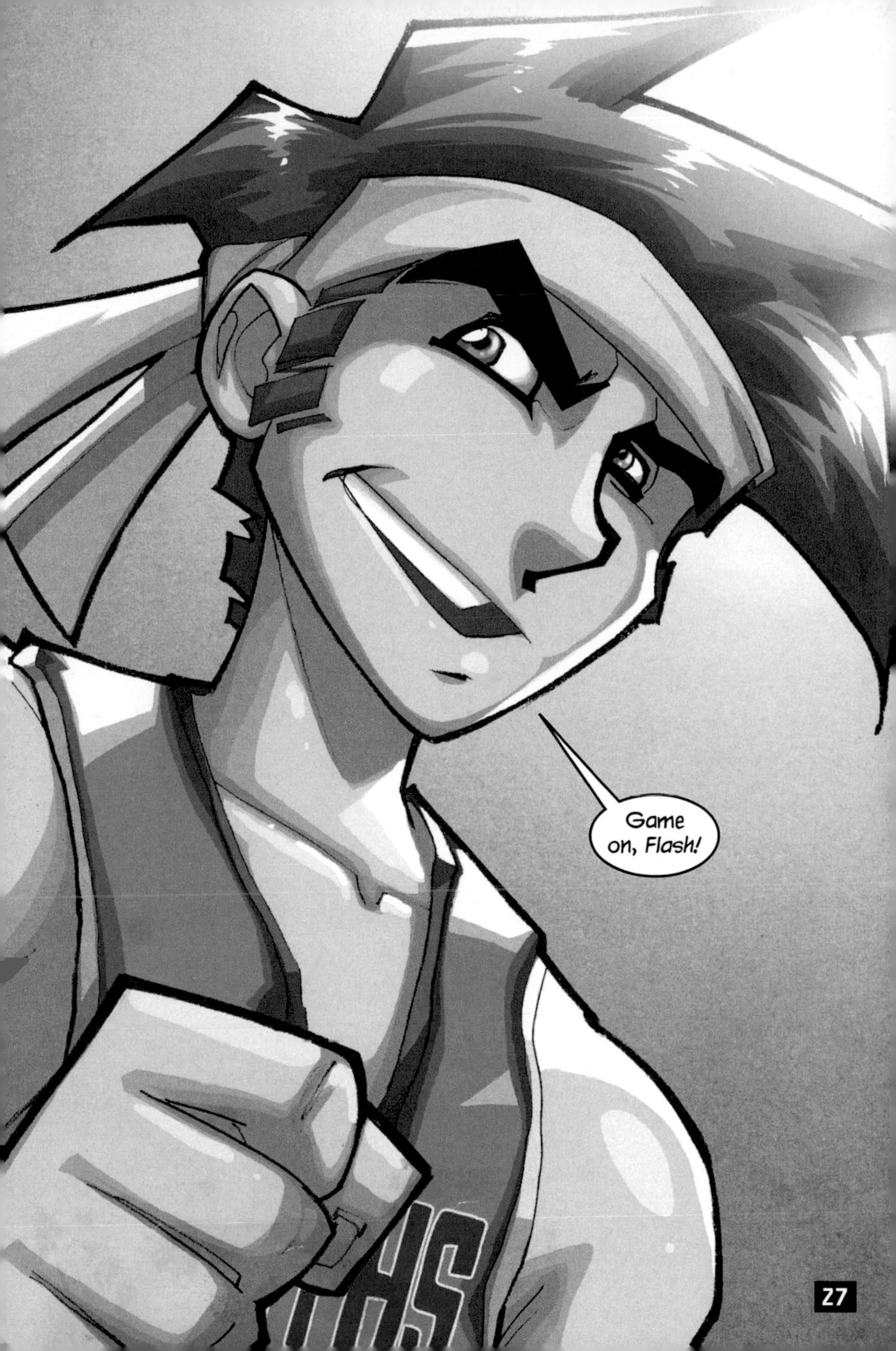
Game on, Flash!

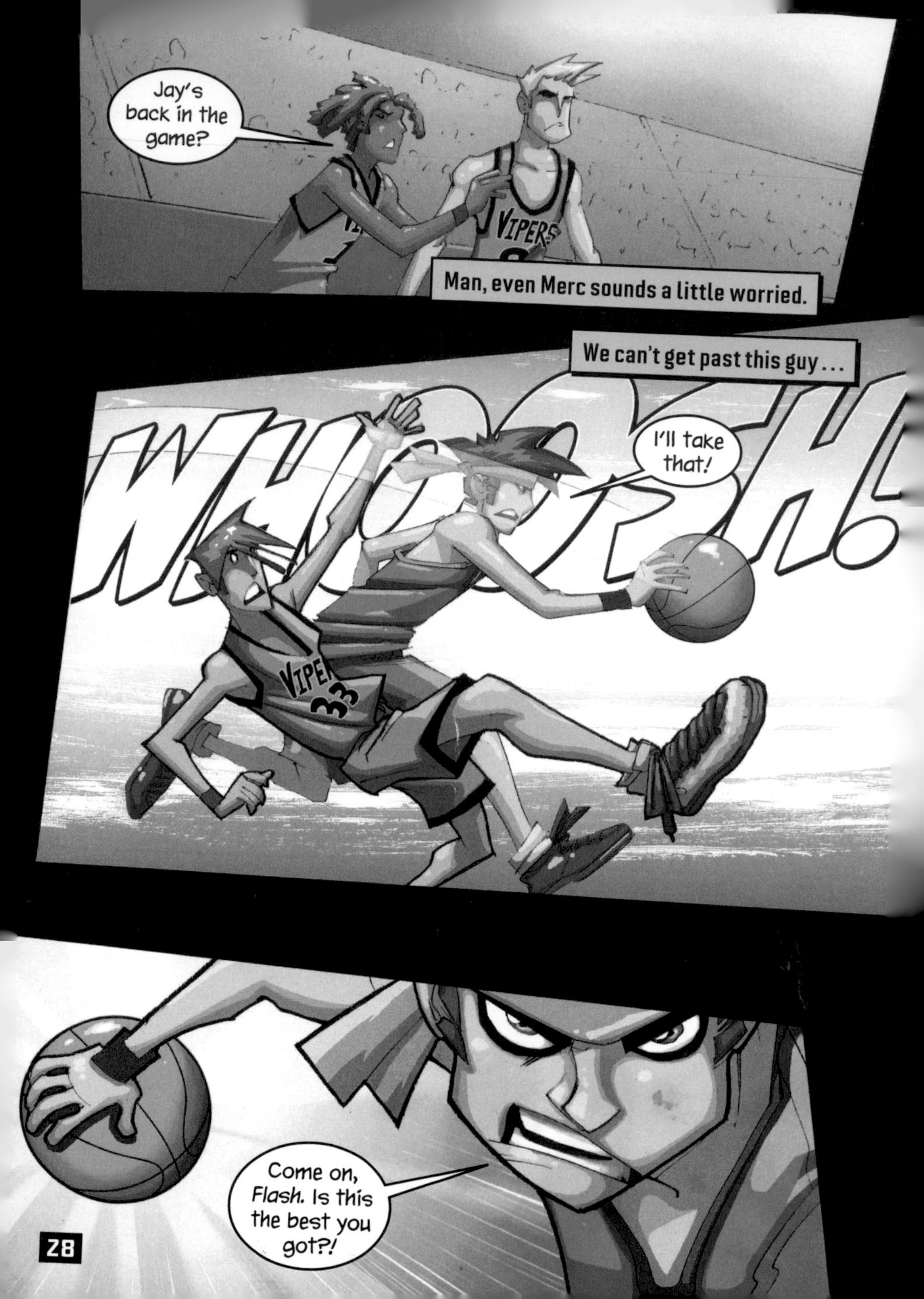
Jay's back in the game?
Man, even Merc sounds a little worried.
We can't get past this guy . . .
WHOOSH!
I'll take that!
VIPERS
33
Come on, Flash. Is this the best you got?!

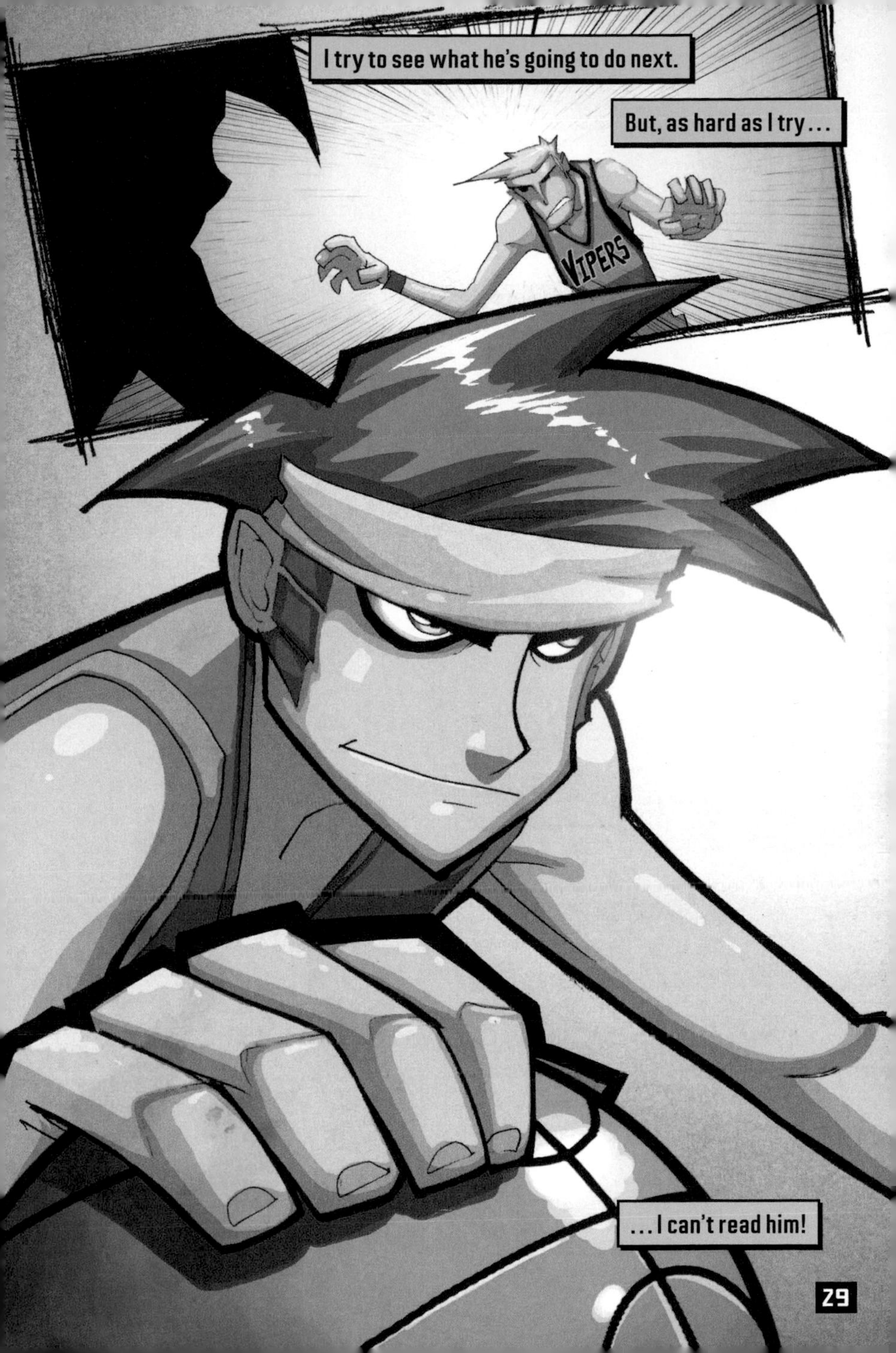
I try to see what he's going to do next.
But, as hard as I try...
VIPERS
...I can't read him!

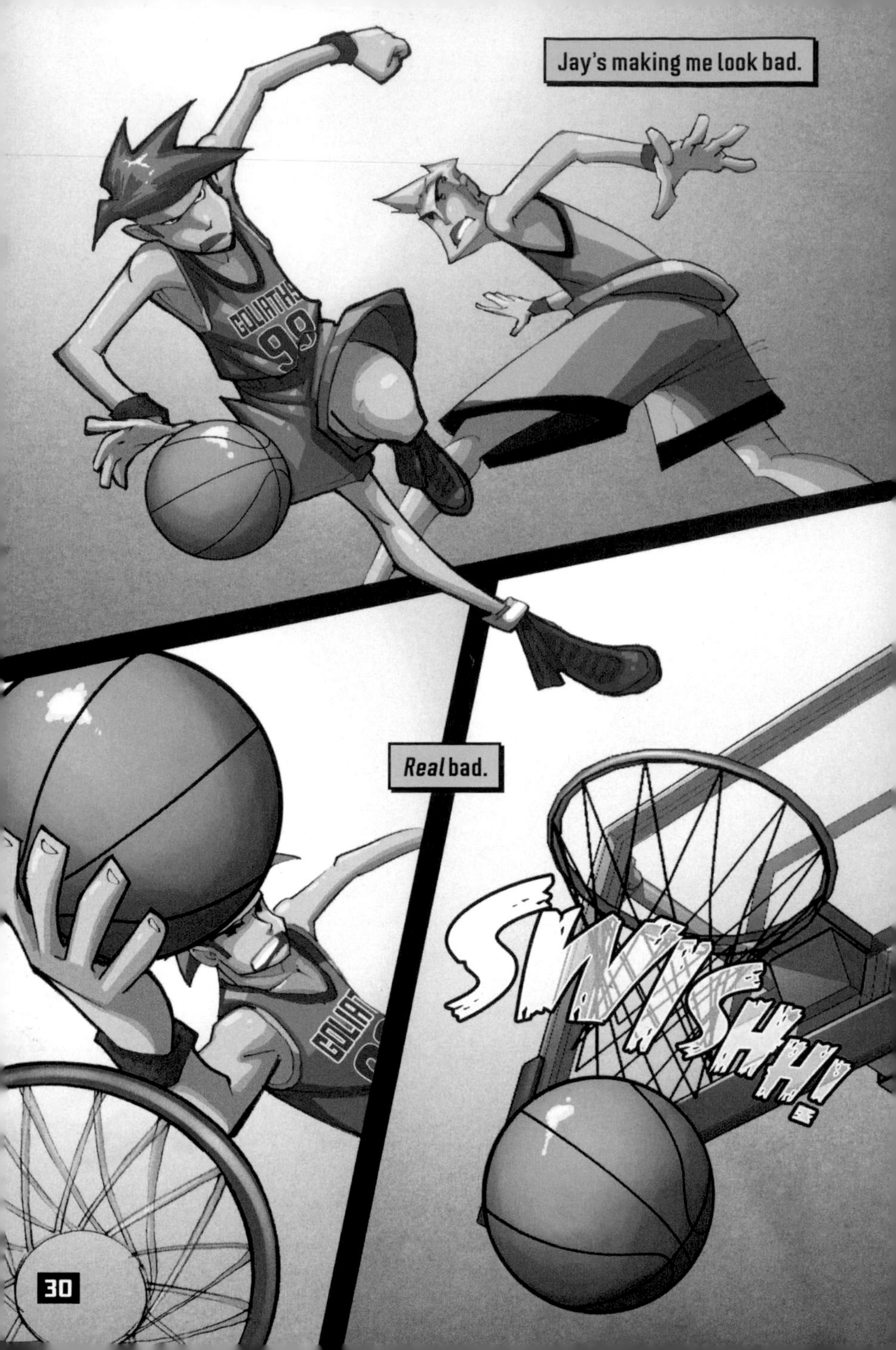
Jay's making me look bad.
GOLIATHS
99
Real bad.
GOLIATHS
SWISHH!

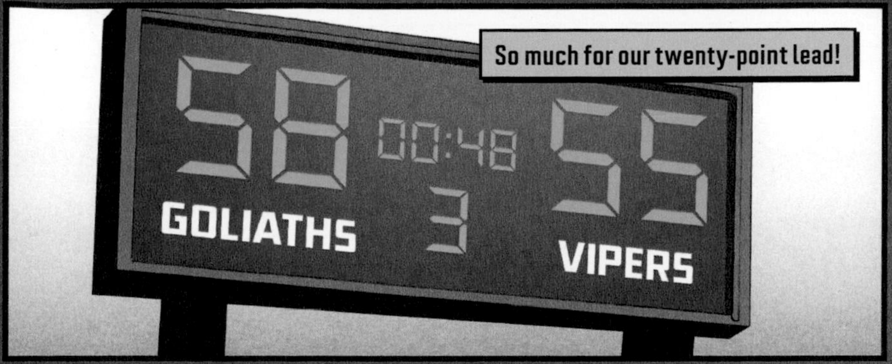
So much for our twenty-point lead!
58
00:48
55
GOLIATHS
3
VIPERS

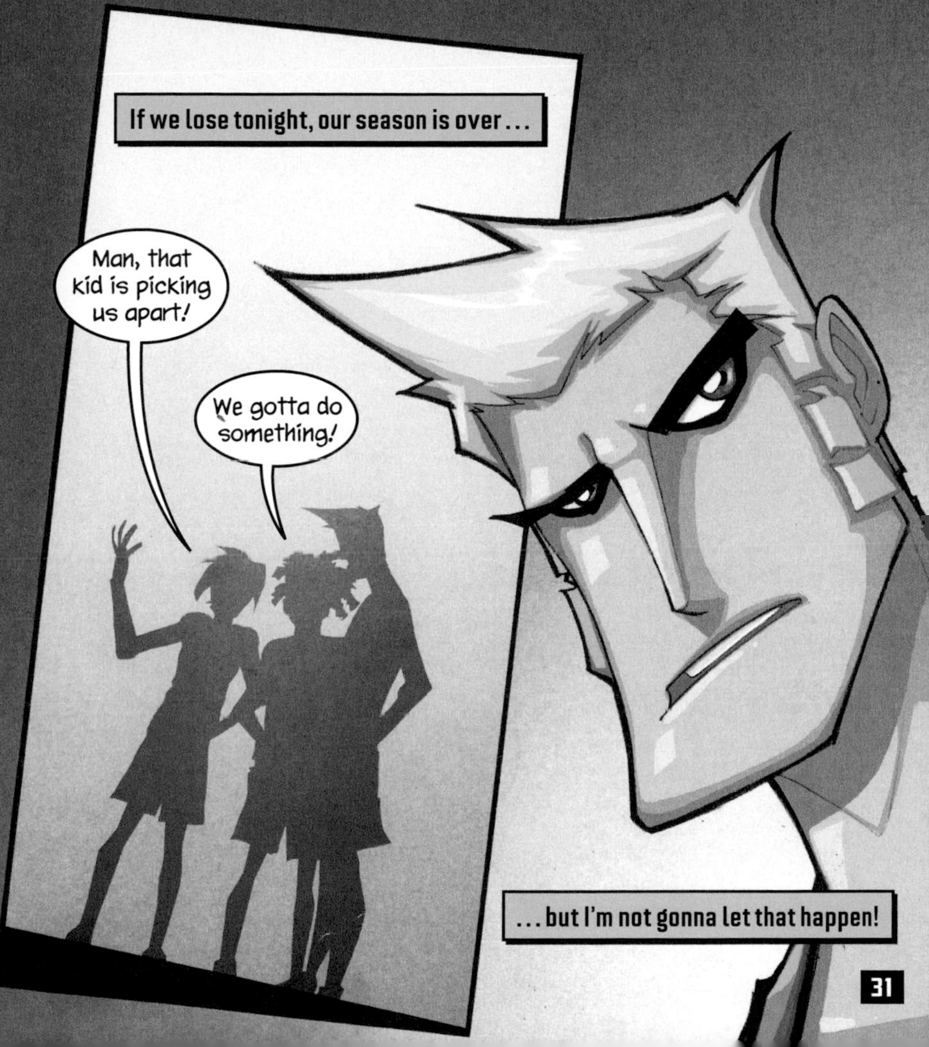
If we lose tonight, our season is over . . .
Man, that kid is picking us apart!
We gotta do something!
. . . but I'm not gonna let that happen!

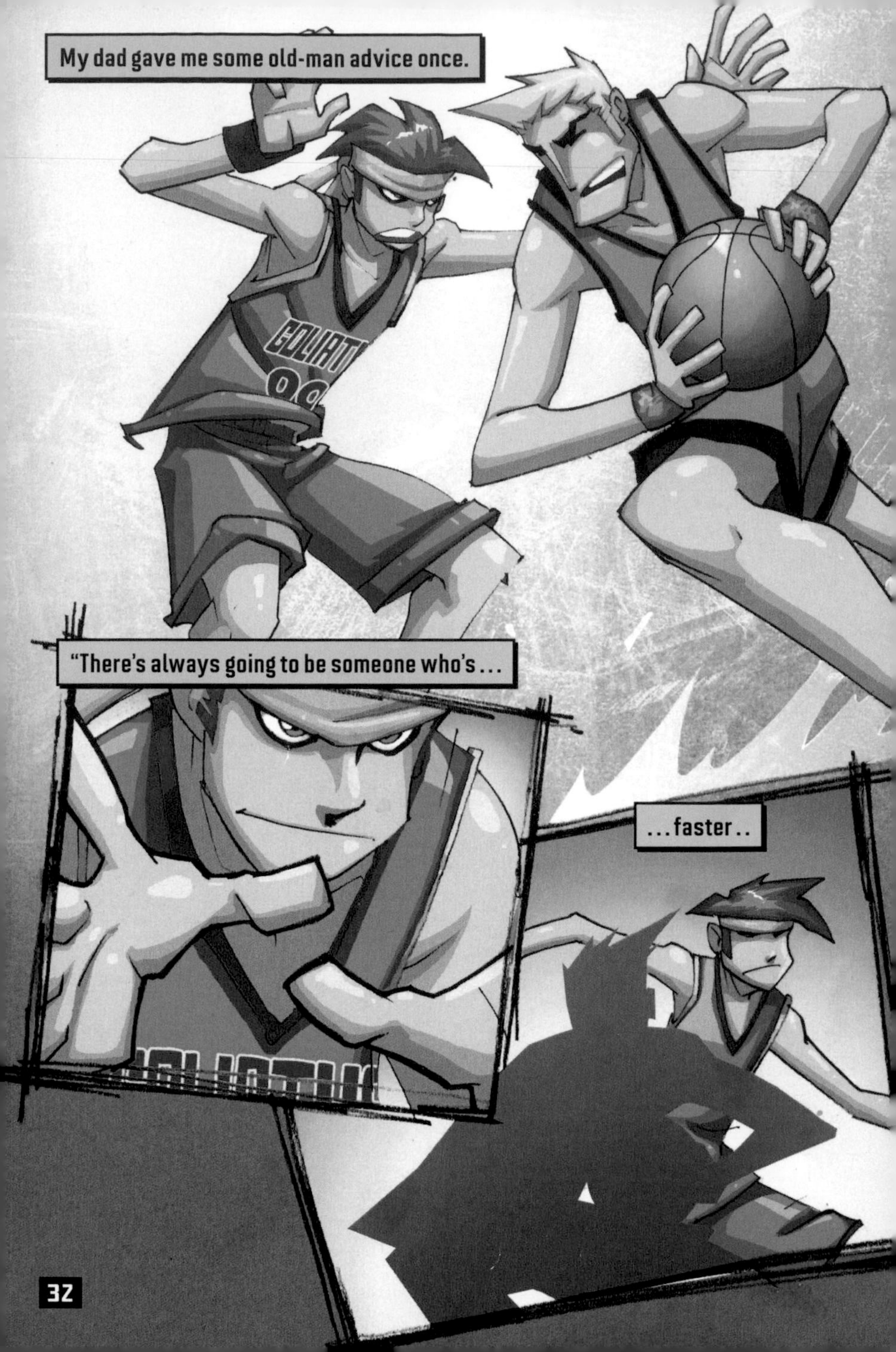
My dad gave me some old-man advice once.
"There's always going to be someone who's . . .
. . . faster . .
GOLIATH

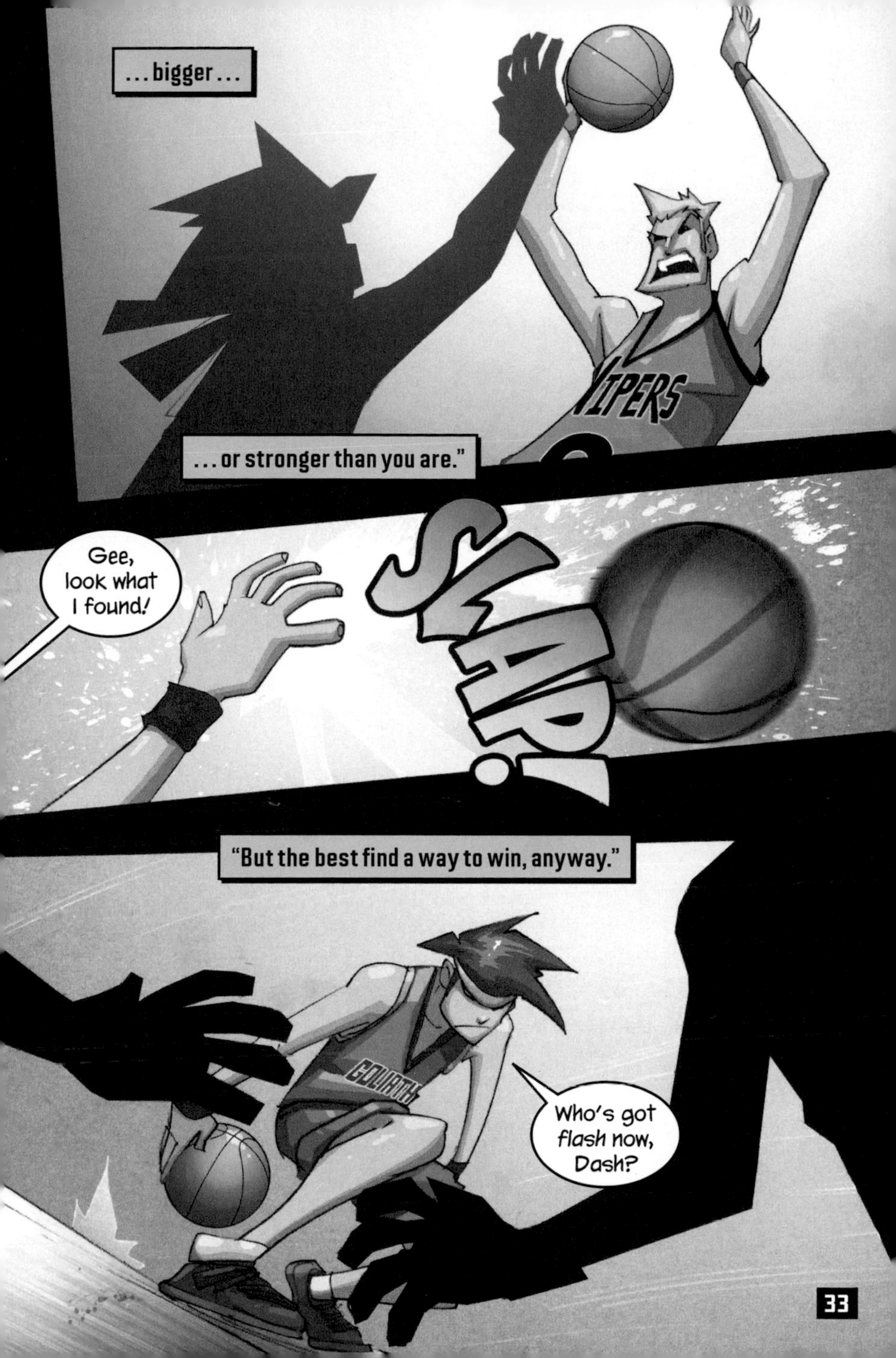

. . . bigger . . .
VIPERS
. . . or stronger than you are."
Gee, look what I found!
SLAP!
"But the best find a way to win, anyway."
GOLIATHS
Who's got flash now, Dash?

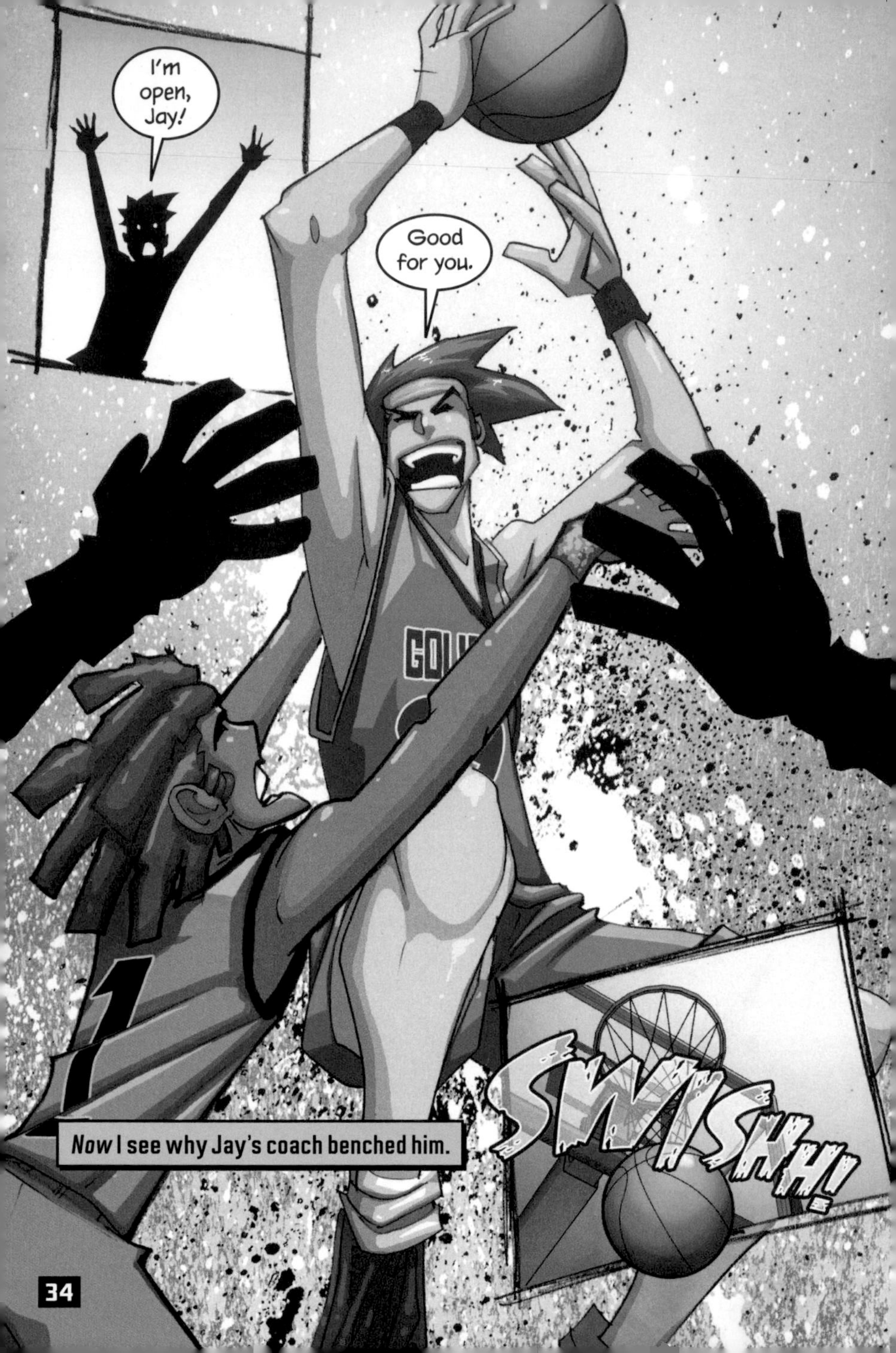
I'm open, Jay!
Good for you.
SWISHH!
Now I see why Jay's coach benched him.

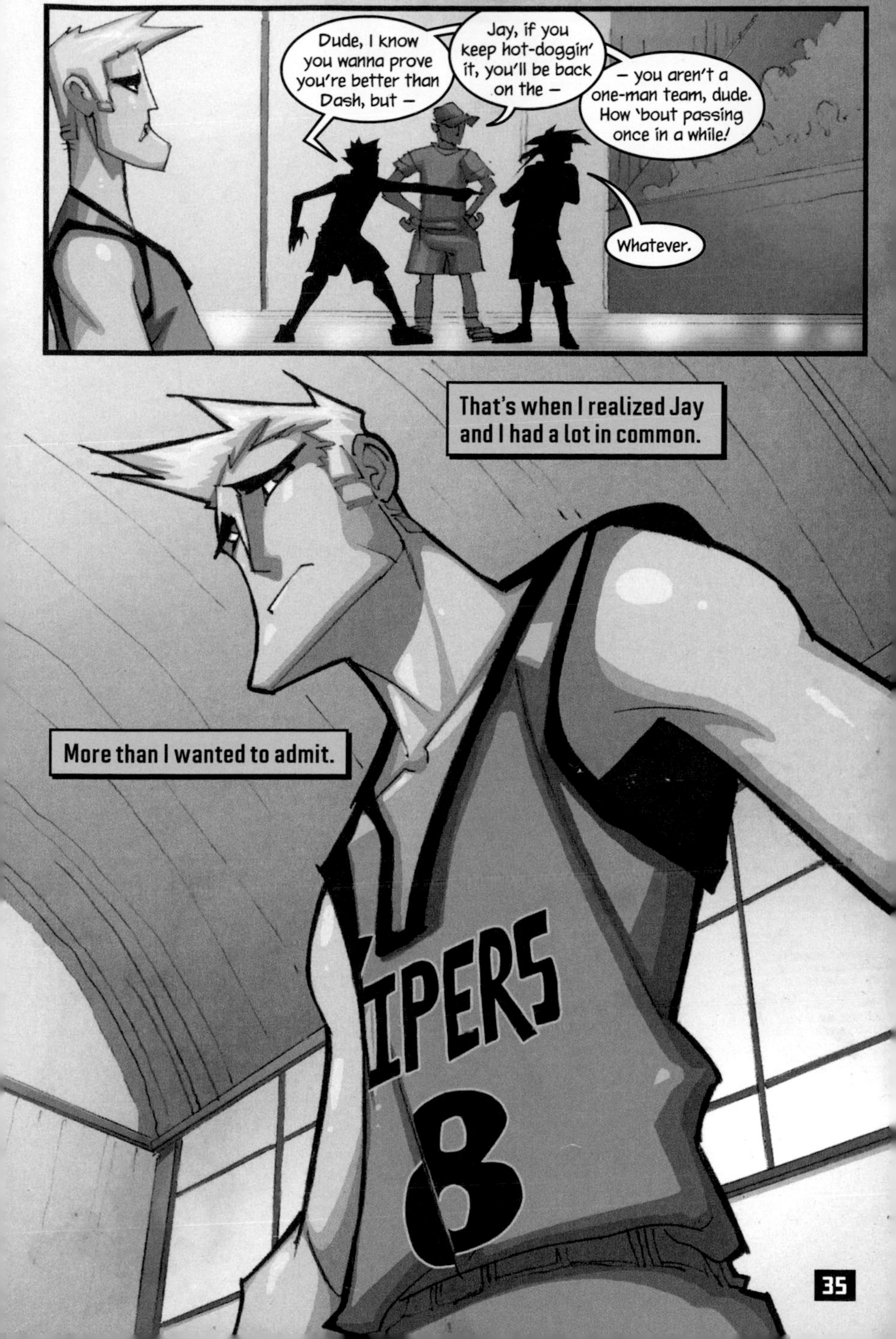
Dude, I know you wanna prove you're better than Dash, but —
Jay, if you keep hot-doggin' it, you'll be back on the —
— you aren't a one-man team, dude. How 'bout passing once in a while!
Whatever.
That's when I realized Jay and I had a lot in common.
More than I wanted to admit.
IPERS
8

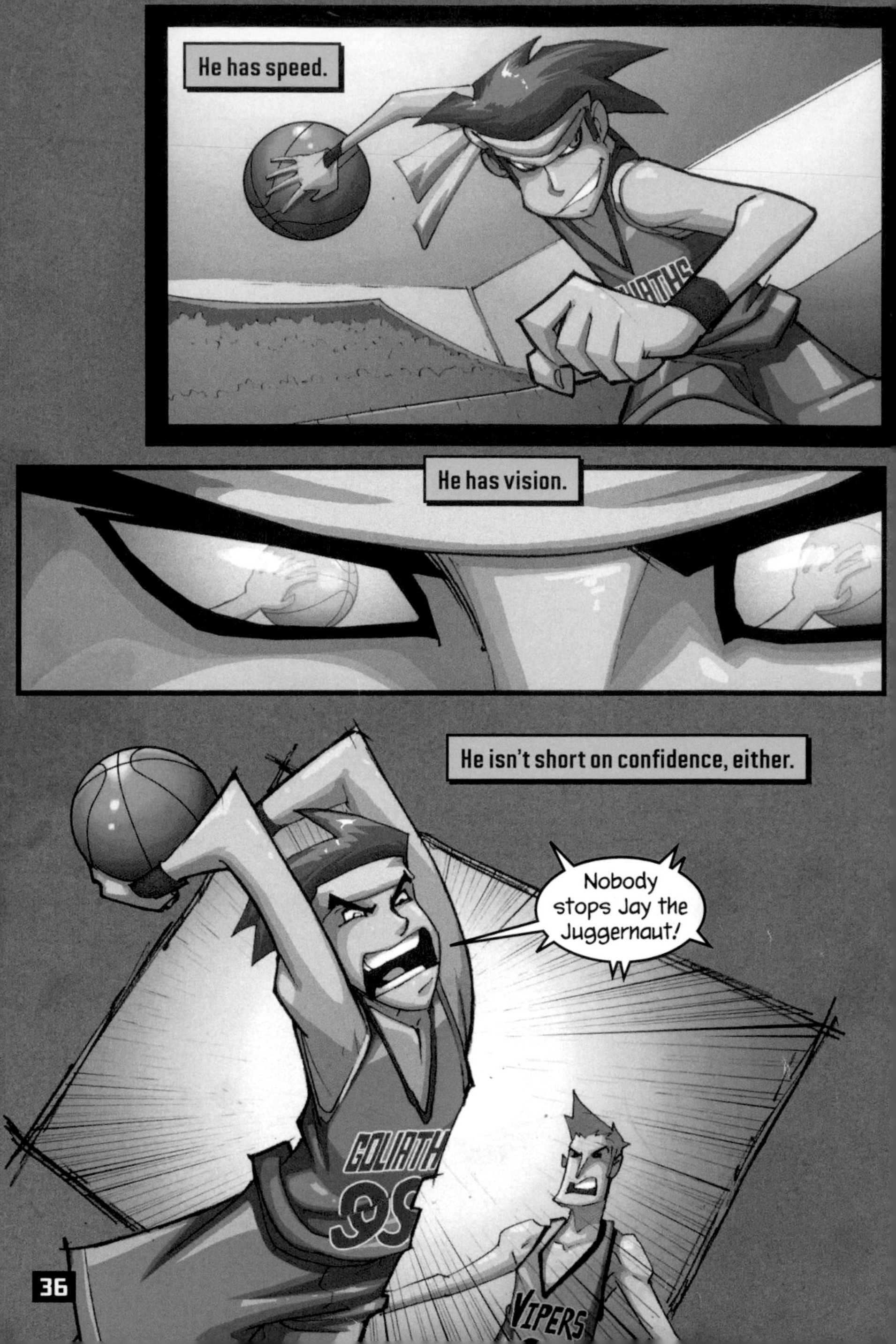
He has speed.
He has vision.
He isn't short on confidence, either.
Nobody stops Jay the Juggernaut!
VIPERS

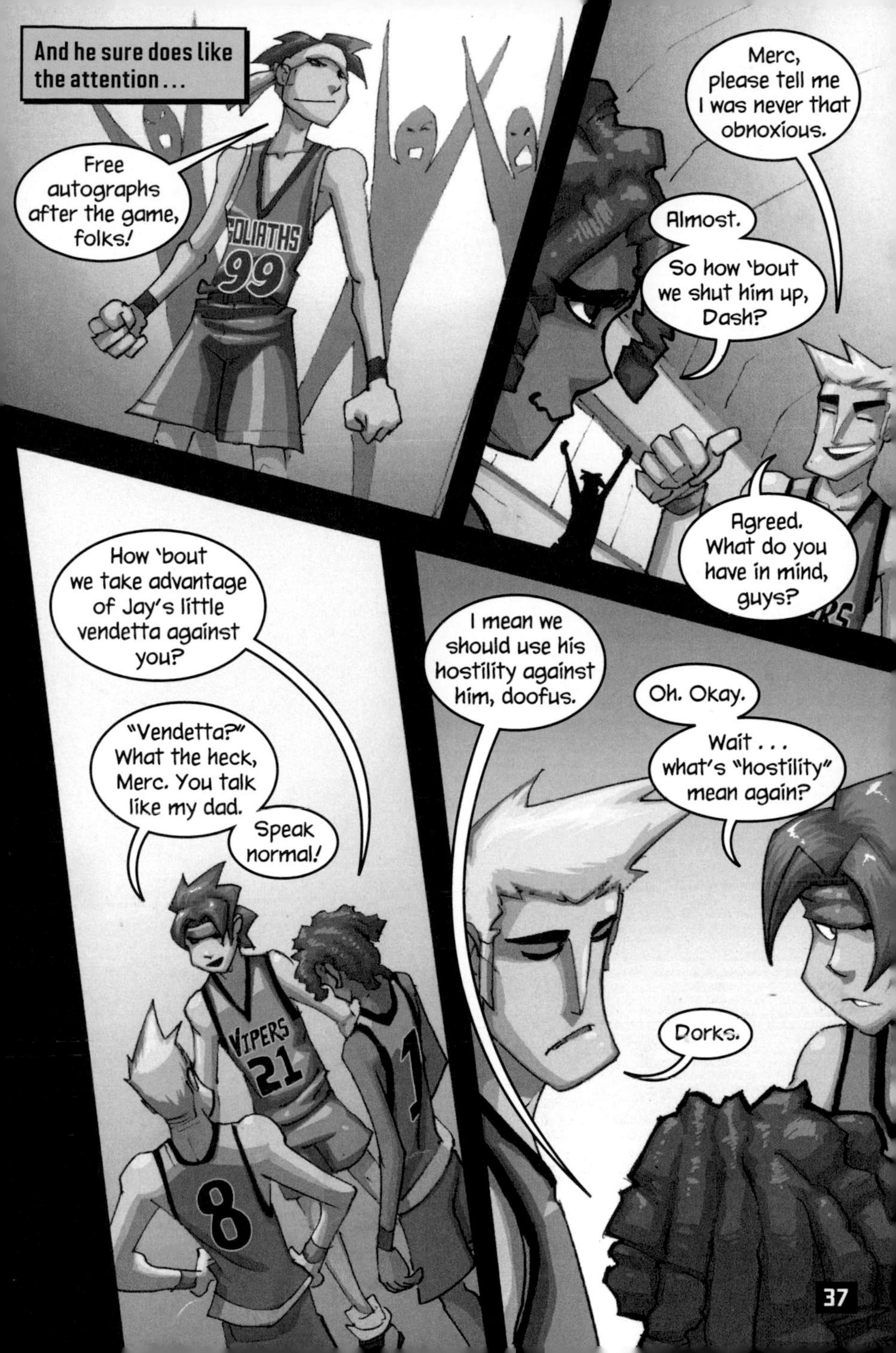
And he sure does like the attention . . .
Free autographs after the game, folks!
GOLIATHS 99
Merc, please tell me I was never that obnoxious.
Almost.
So how 'bout we shut him up, Dash?
Agreed. What do you have in mind, guys?
How 'bout we take advantage of Jay's little vendetta against you?
"Vendetta?" What the heck, Merc. You talk like my dad.
Speak normal!
VIPERS 21
I mean we should use his hostility against him, doofus.
Oh. Okay.
Wait . . . what's "hostility" mean again?
Dorks.

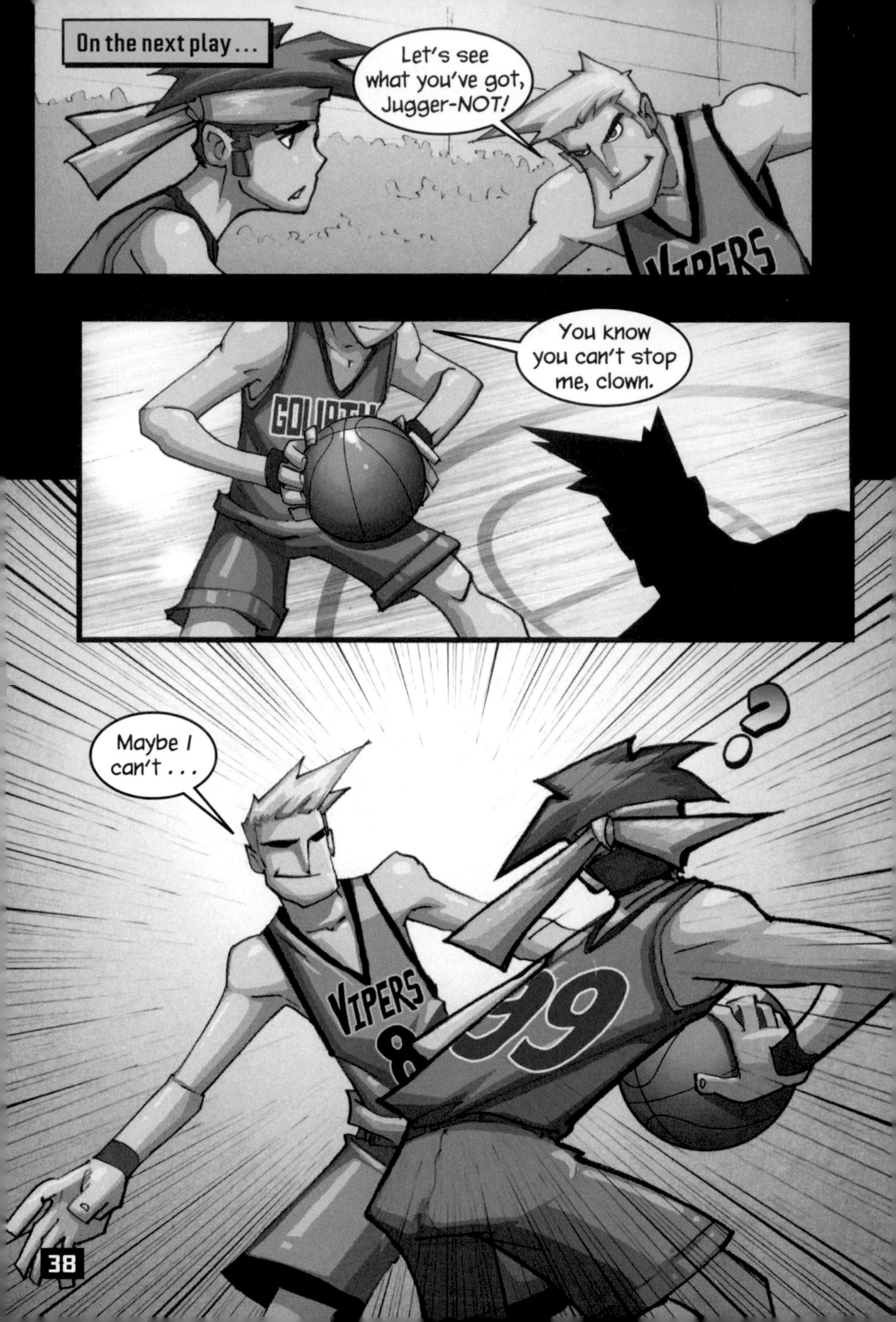

On the next play . . .
Let's see what you've got, Jugger-NOT!
VIPERS
You know you can't stop me, clown.
Maybe I can't . . .
?
VIPERS
8
99

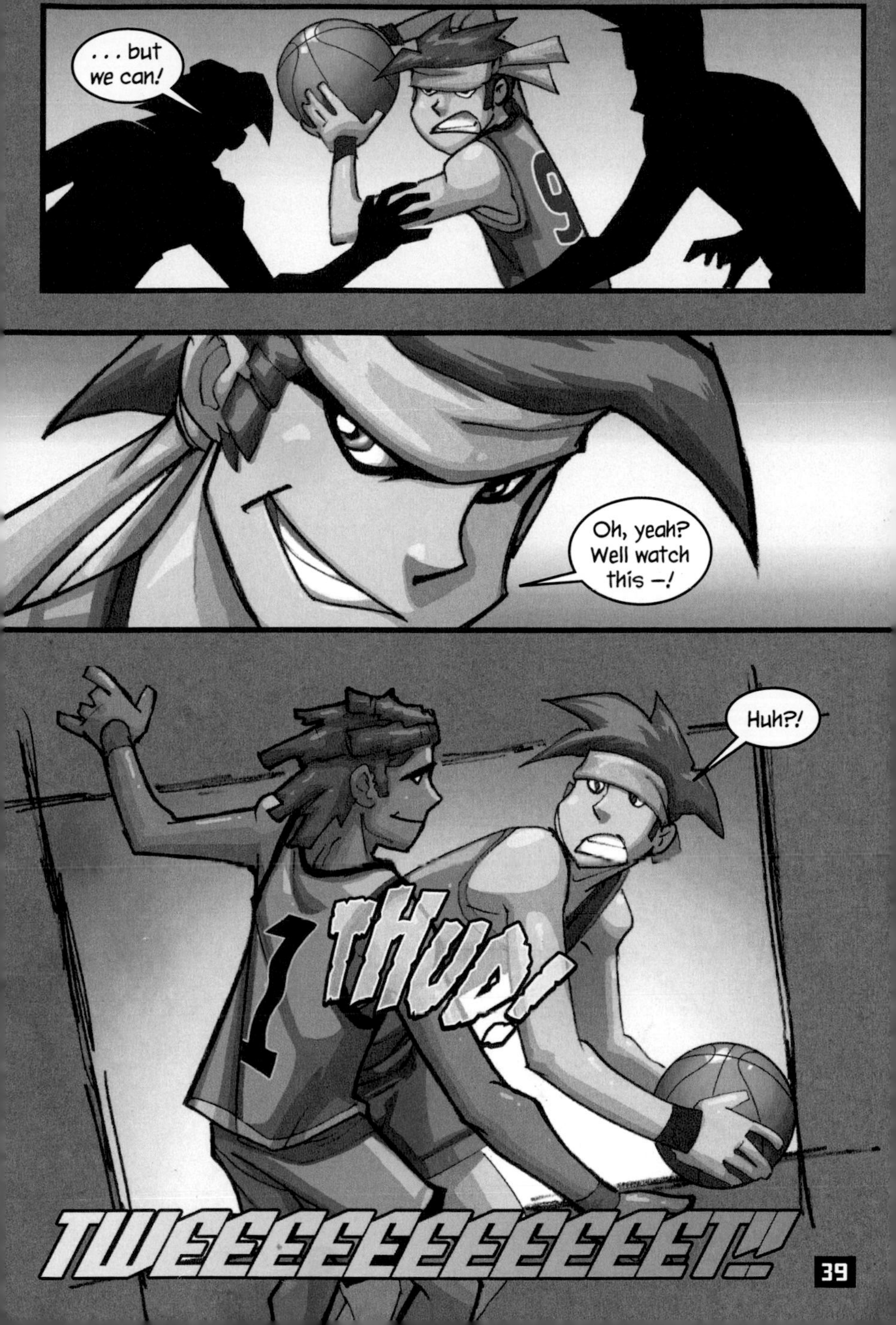
. . . but we can!
Oh, yeah? Well watch this —!
Huh?!
THUD!
TWEEEEEEEEEEEEET!!

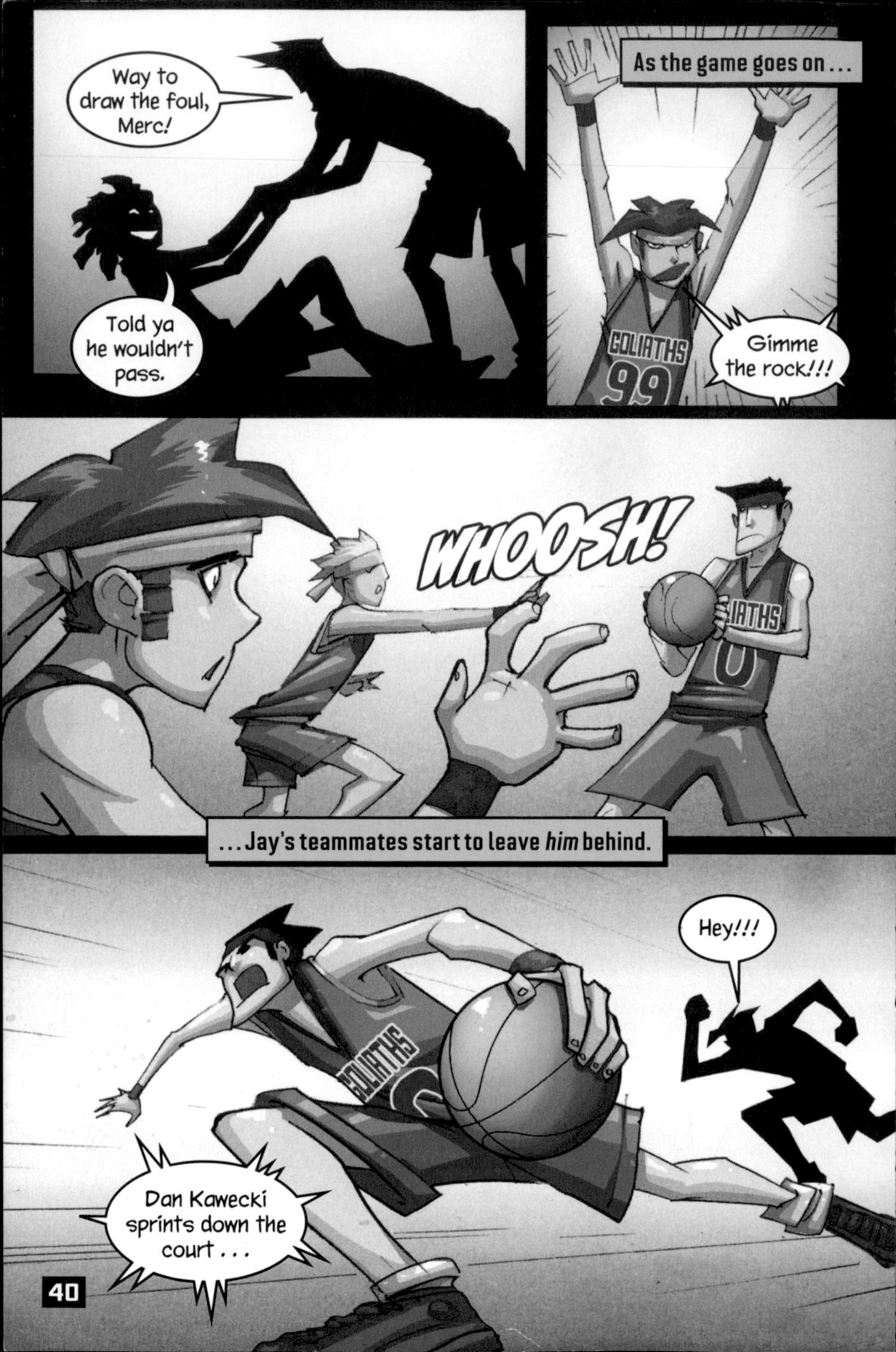

Way to draw the foul, Merc!
Told ya he wouldn't pass.
As the game goes on . . .
GOLIATHS 99
Gimme the rock!!!
WHOOSH!
. . . Jay's teammates start to leave *him* behind.
Hey!!!
GOLIATHS
Dan Kawecki sprints down the court . . .

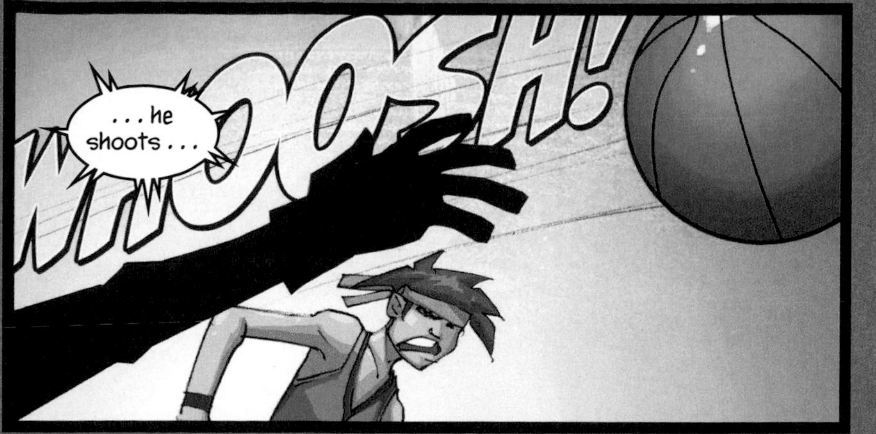
WHOOOSH!
. . . he shoots . . .

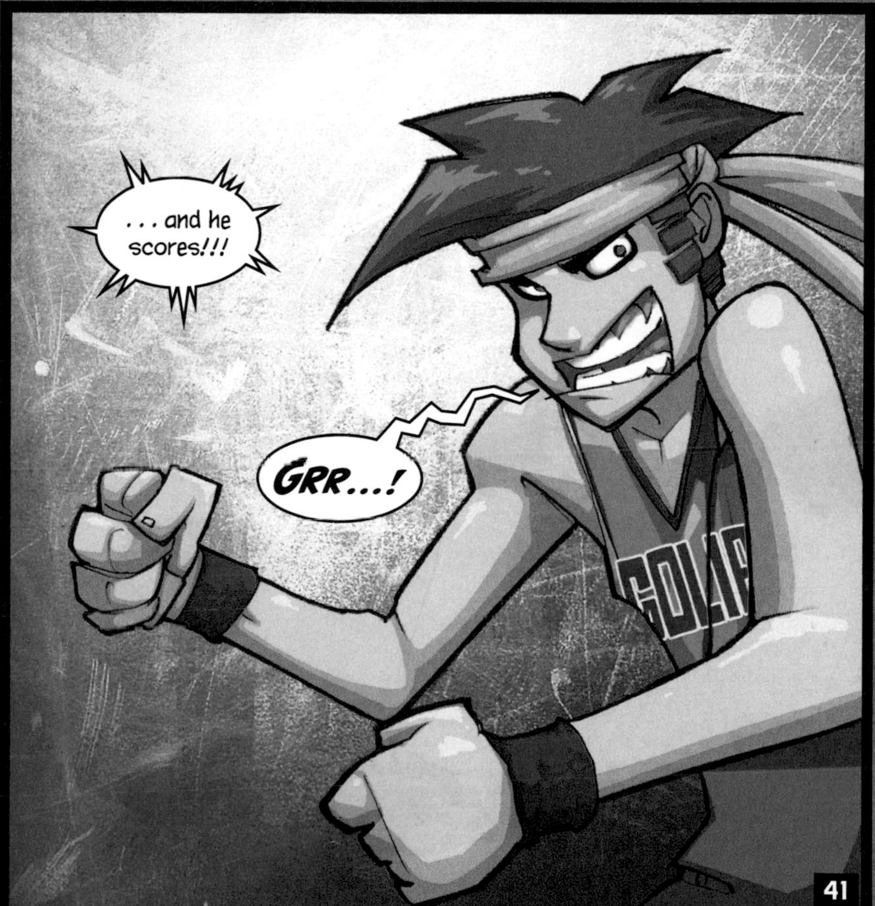
. . . and he scores!!!
GRR...!

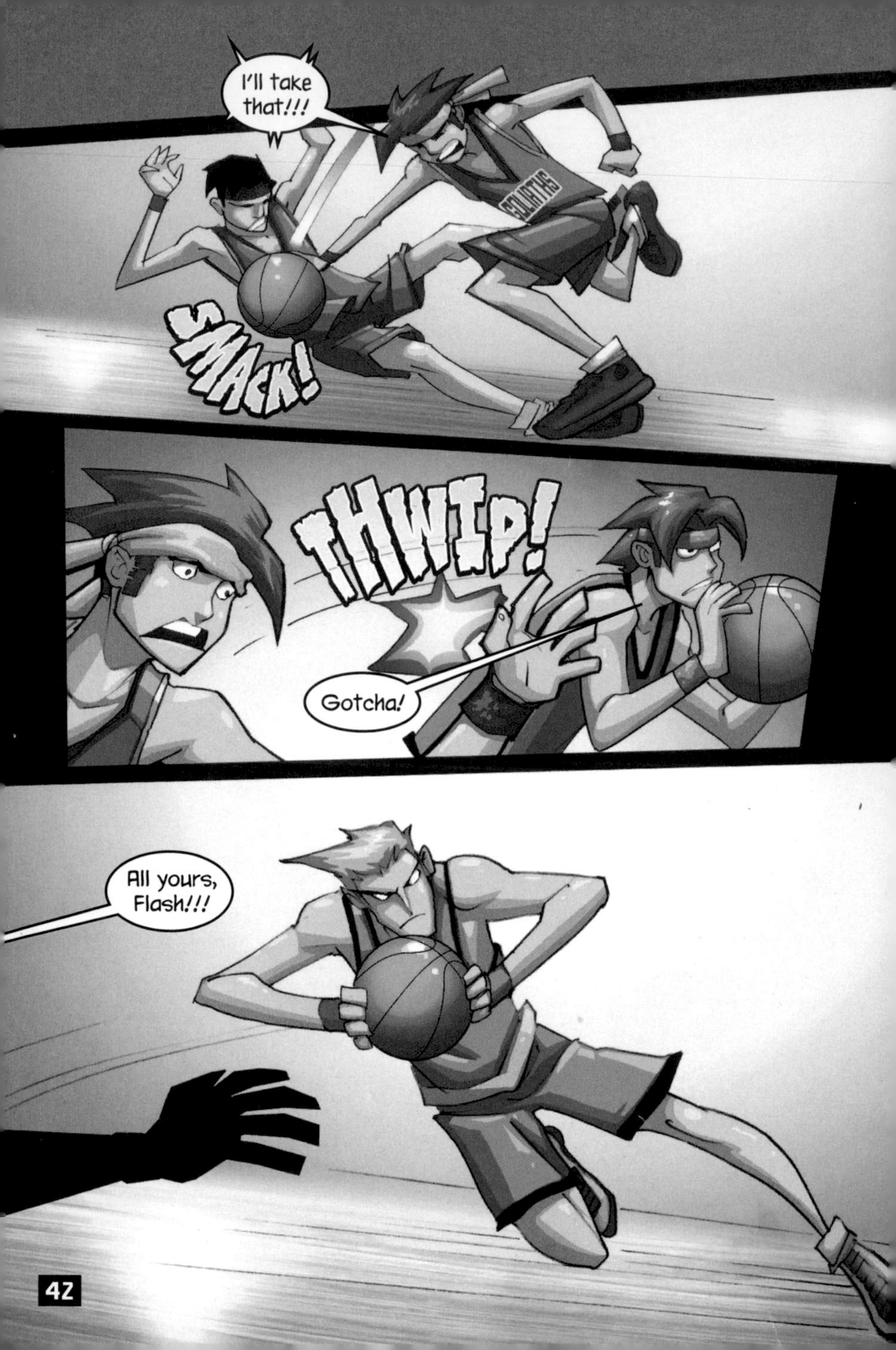
I'll take that!!!
GOLIATHS
SMACK!
THWIP!
Gotcha!
All yours, Flash!!!

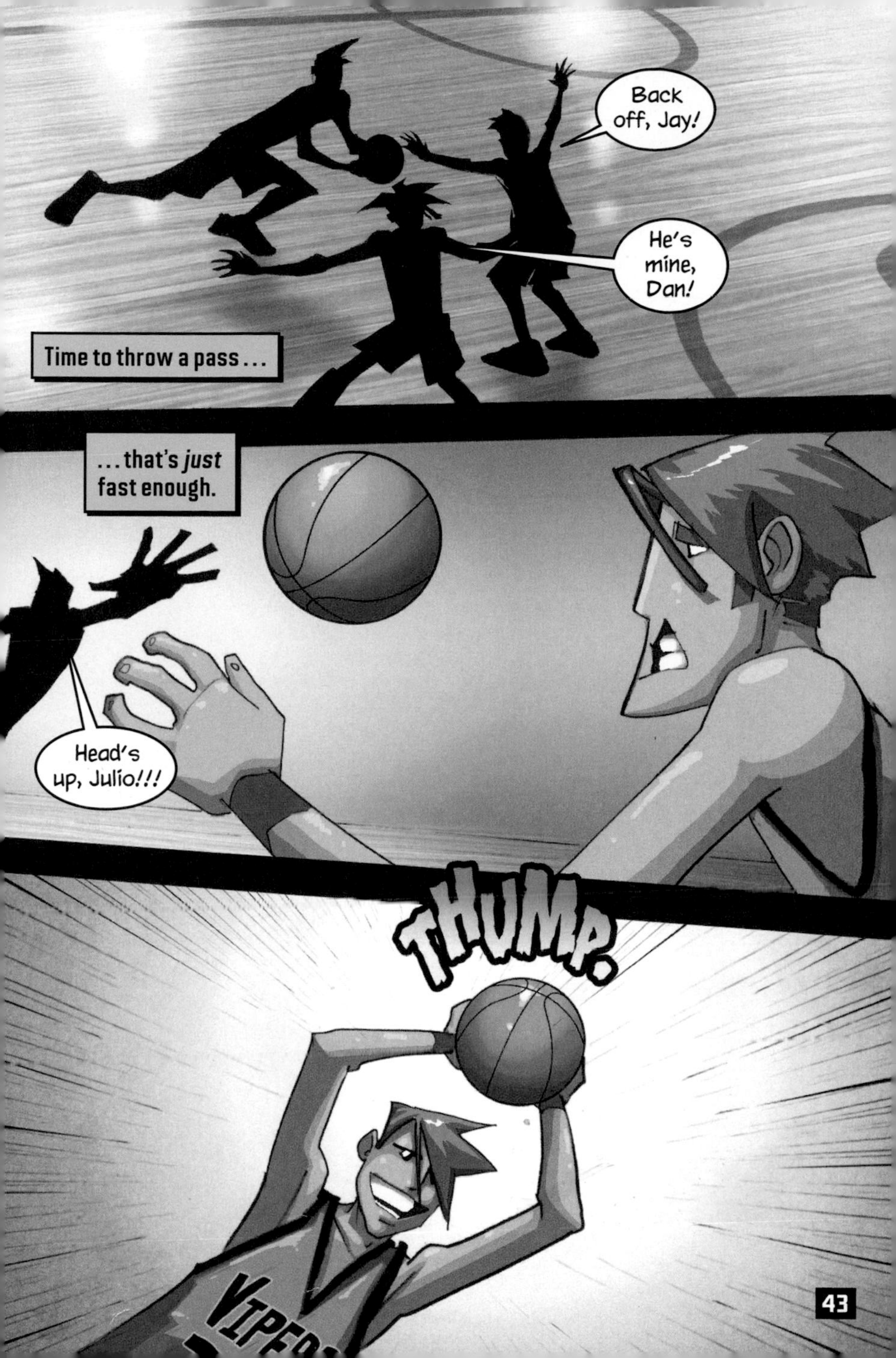

Back off, Jay!
He's mine, Dan!
Time to throw a pass . . .
. . . that's *just* fast enough.
Head's up, Julio!!!
THUMP.

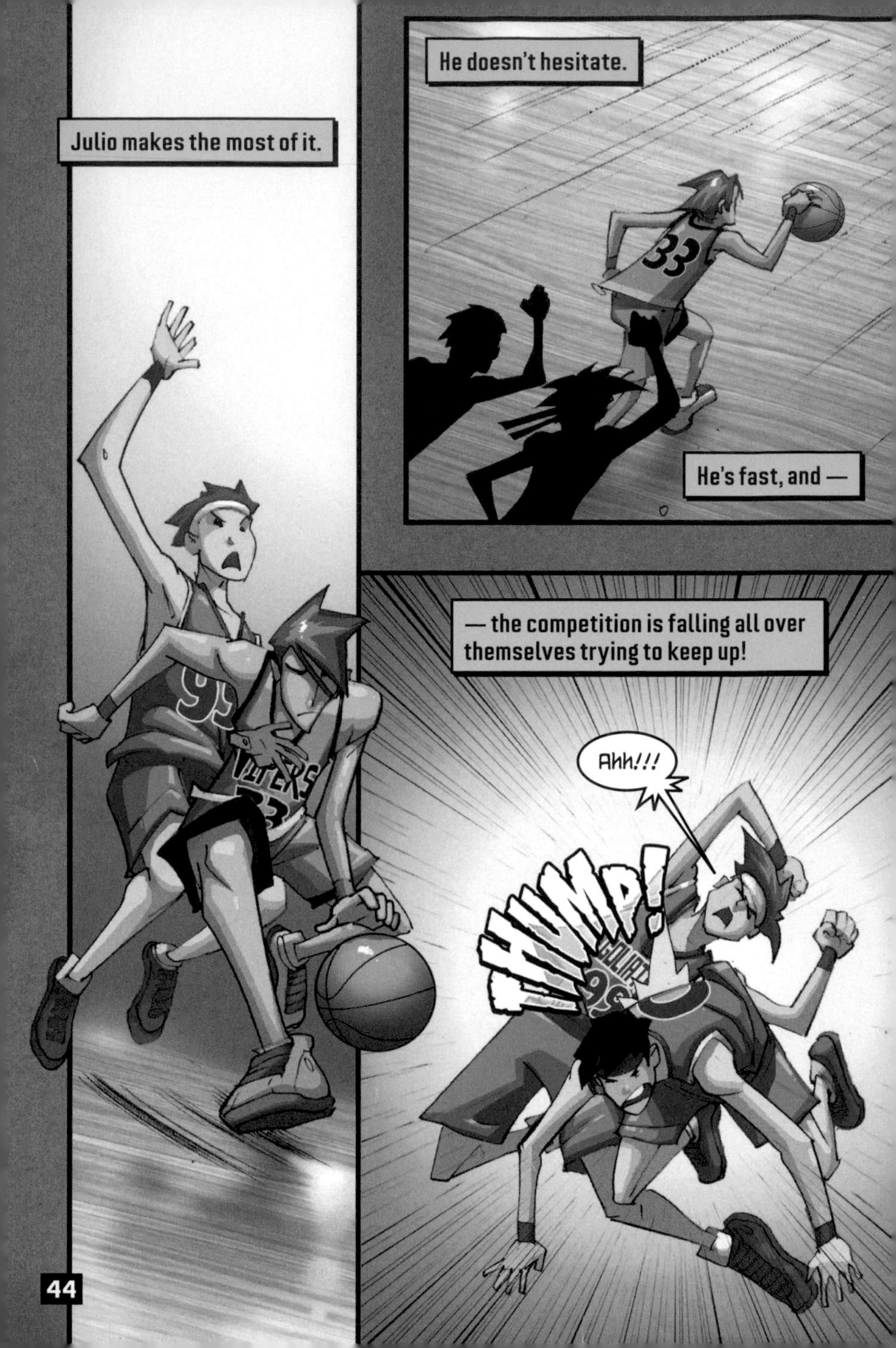
Julio makes the most of it.
He doesn't hesitate.
He's fast, and —
— the competition is falling all over themselves trying to keep up!
Ahh!!!
THUMP!

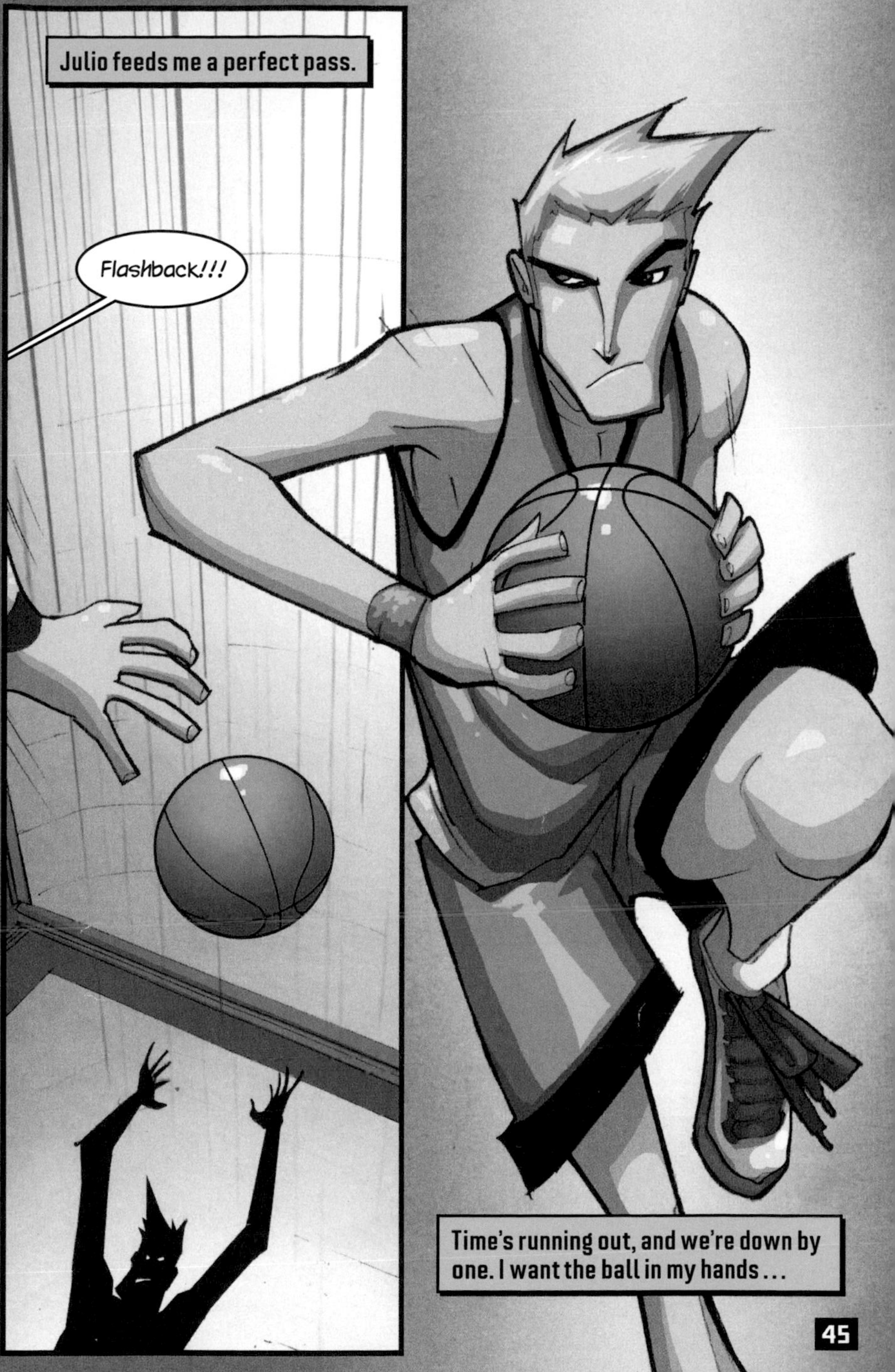
Julio feeds me a perfect pass.
Flashback!!!
Time's running out, and we're down by one. I want the ball in my hands . . .

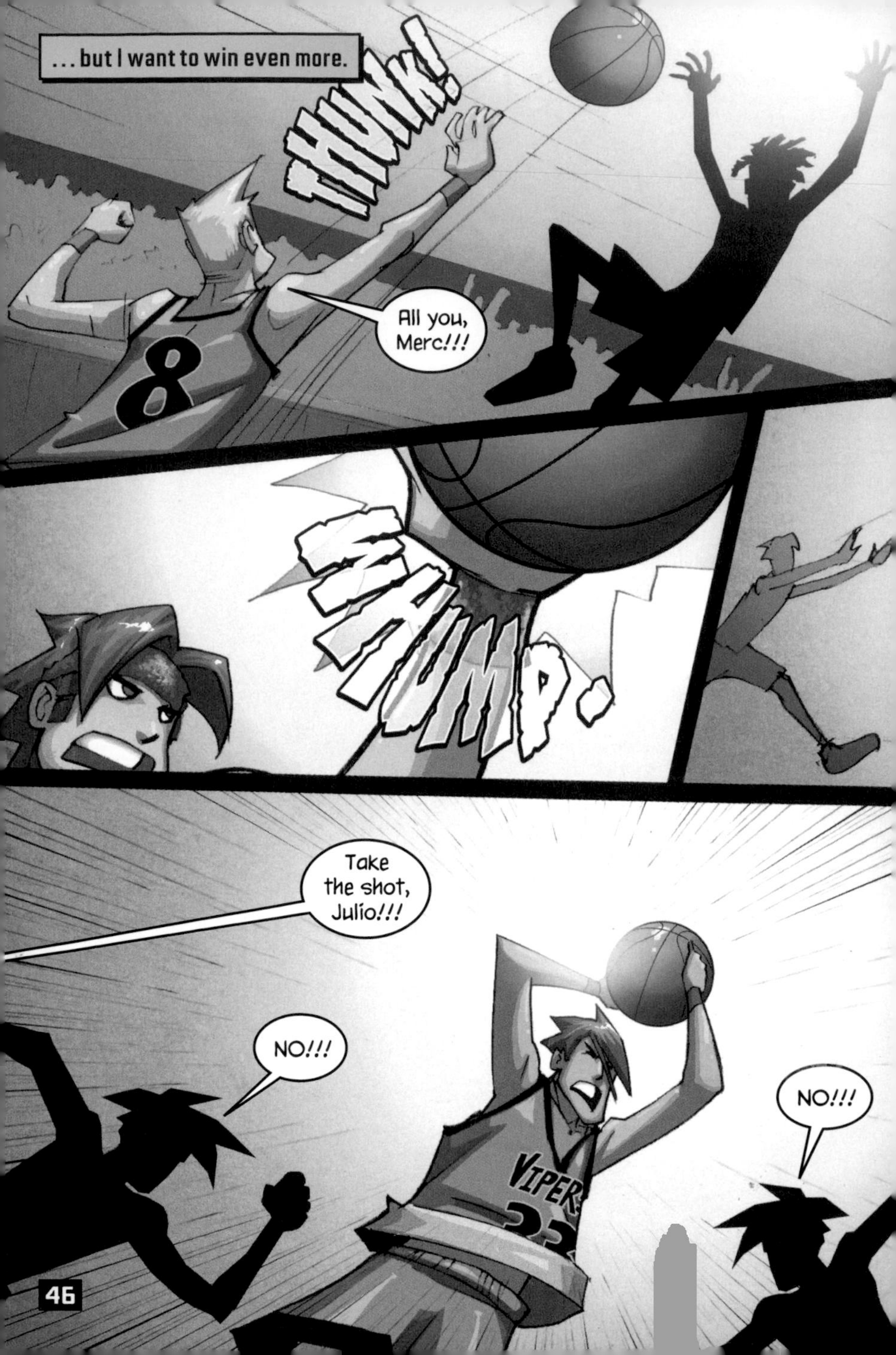

... but I want to win even more.
THUNK!
All you, Merc!!!
THUMP!
Take the shot, Julio!!!
NO!!!
NO!!!
VIPERS

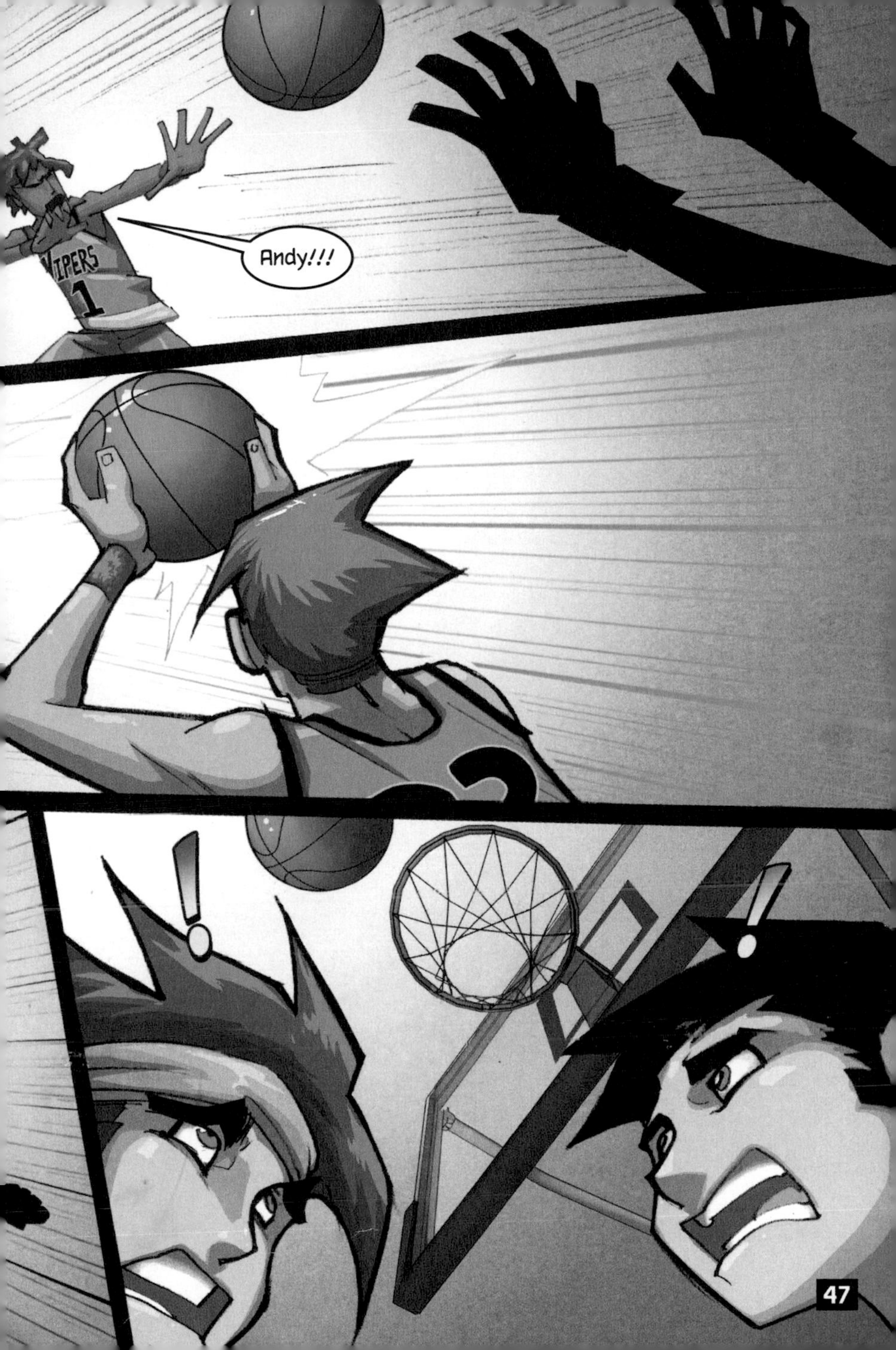
VIPERS
1
Andy!!!
!
!

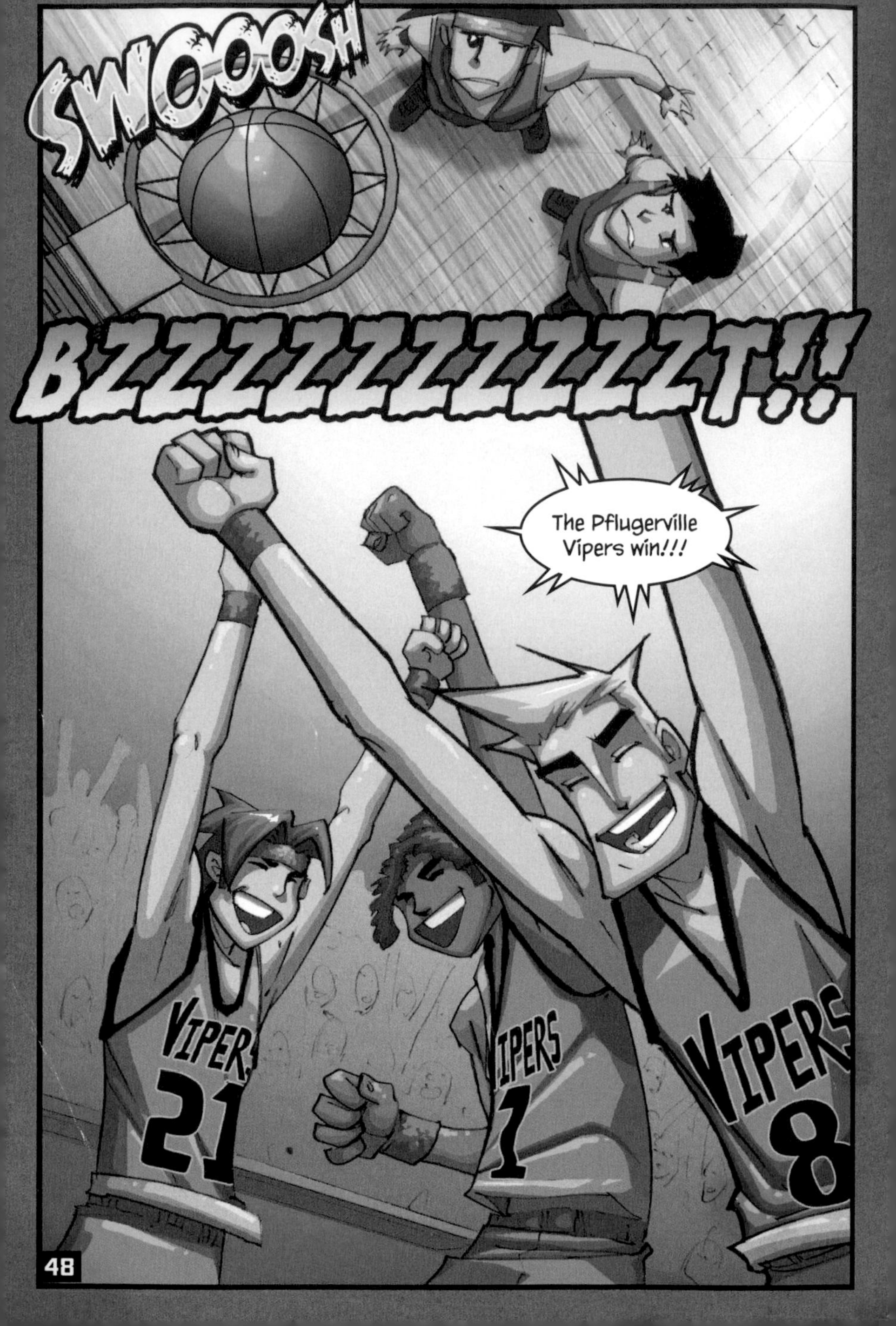
SWOOOSH
BZZZZZZZZZZZZT!!
The Pflugerville Vipers win!!!
VIPERS 21
VIPERS 1
VIPERS 8

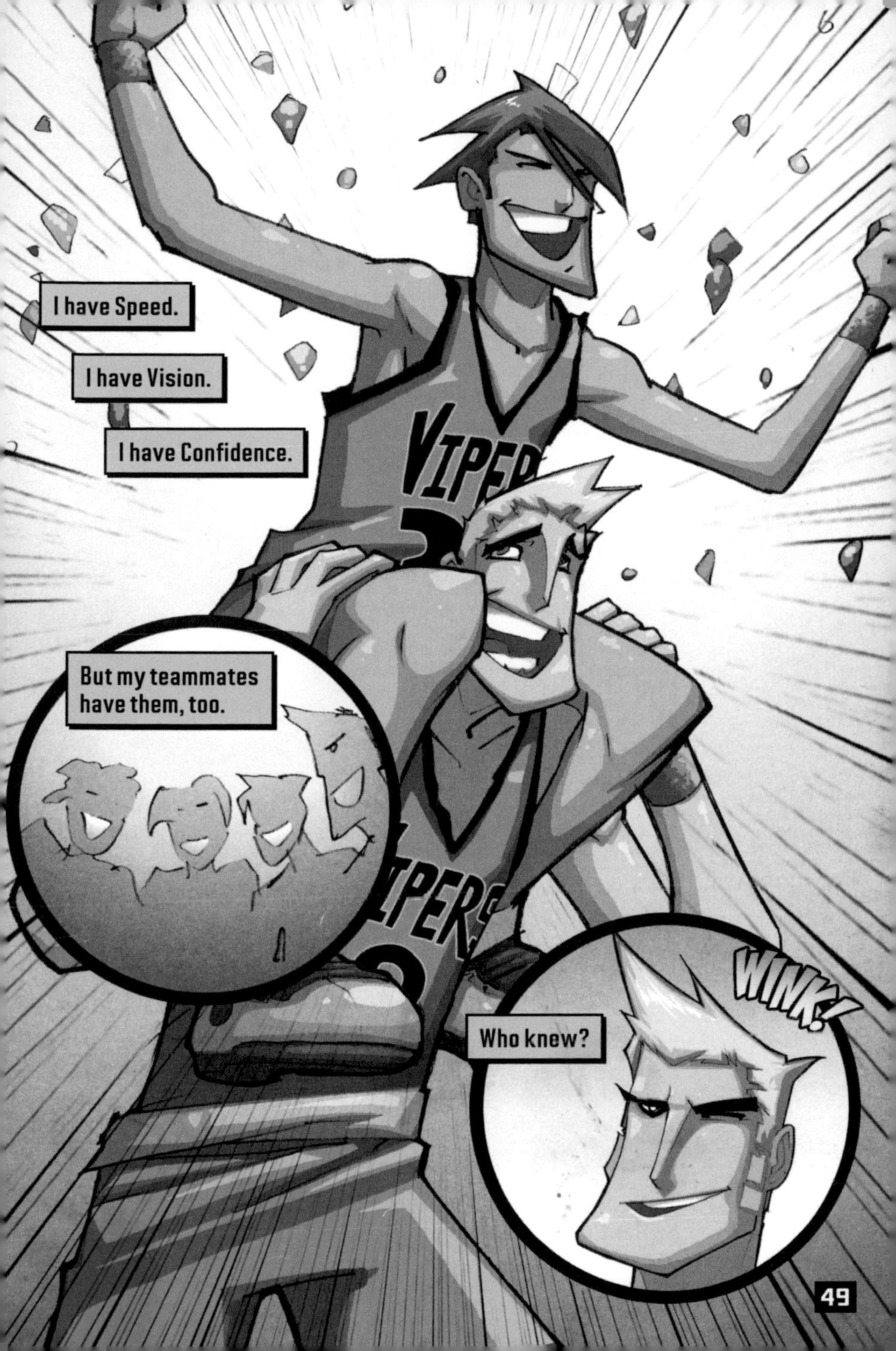
I have Speed.
I have Vision.
I have Confidence.
VIPERS
But my teammates have them, too.
VIPERS
WINK!
Who knew?

SPORTS ZONE

POSTGAME RECAP

BBL
BASKETBALL

PNT
PAINTBALL

FBL
FOOTBALL

BSL
BASEBALL

BBL
BASKETBALL

DASH THE FLASH LEADS VIPERS TO VICTORY!

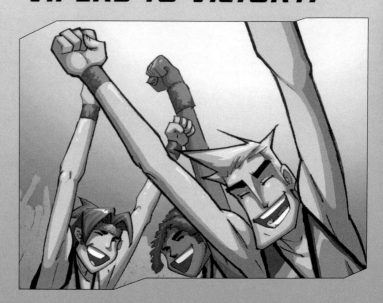

BY THE NUMBERS

POINTS SCORED:
DASH: 27
DAN: 17
JAY: 21

STORY: Dash may have Flash, and he may have led the Vipers in points scored, but Julio's the one who came up big when it counted the most. Julio handled himself extremely well on the court and surprised nearly everyone when he sank the game-winning shot! Dash said, "I always knew Julio had talent — but I never knew he had flash, too!"

Sports Illustrated KIDS

UP NEXT: SI KIDS INFO CENTER

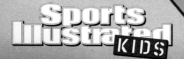

SZ POSTGAME EXTRA

WHERE ***YOU*** ANALYZE THE GAME!

BLZ vs BKS 3-1
TGR vs RDR 33-32
EAG vs BAN 14-7
SPA vs WLD 4-3
BAN vs RDR 21-15
RZR vs LIG 4-3
BLZ vs BKS 3-1

Basketball fans got a real treat today when Jay the Juggernat faced off against Dash the Flash. Let's go into the stands and ask some fans for their opinions on the day's big game . . .

DISCUSSION QUESTION 1

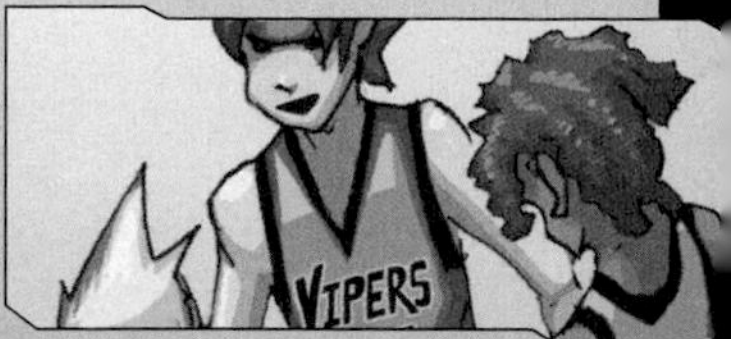
VIPERS

Which player was your favorite — Merc, Andy, Julio, Dash, Dan, or Jay? Why?

DISCUSSION QUESTION 2

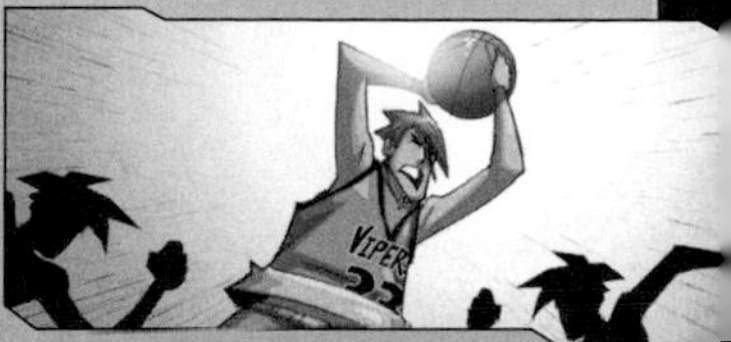

What position is the most difficult to play in basketball, and why?

WRITING PROMPT 1

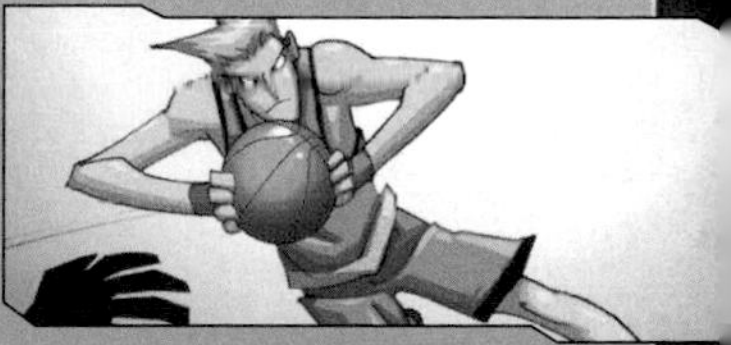

What kinds of skills or qualities make for a good center? How about for a good point guard? Which position would you be best at? Write about basketball positions.

WRITING PROMPT 2

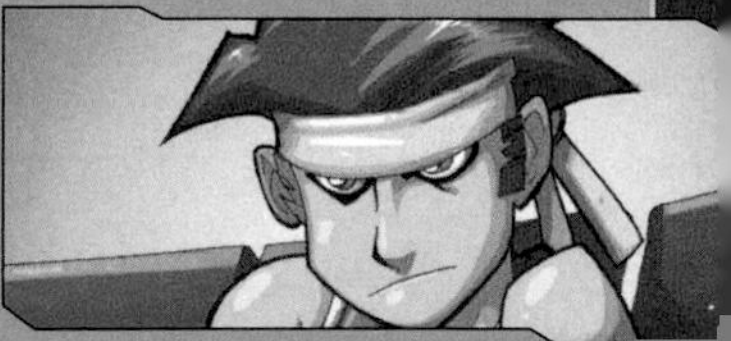

Do you think Jay is a good kid, a bad kid, or both? What did Jay do that might make him bad? Write about it.

GLOSSARY

ADVANTAGE   (ad-VAN-tij)—something that helps you or is useful to you

CONFIDENCE   (CON-fuh-duhnss)—if you have confidence, you believe in yourself and your abilities

DECOY   (DEE-koy)—someone who lures a person into a trap or draws attention away from something

HESITATE   (HEZ-uh-tate)—if you hesitate, you pause uncertaintly before doing something

HOSTILITY   (hoss-TIL-uh-tee)—strong hatred or dislike

JUGGERNAUT   (JUHG-ur-nawt)—a powerful force that cannot be stopped

LIABILITY   (LYE-uh-bil-uh-tee)—if something is a liability, it means it is a disadvantage

OBNOXIOUS   (uhb-NOK-shuhss)—very unpleasant, annoying, or offensive

VENDETTA   (ven-DET-uh)—a long-lasting feud between two different groups, individuals, or teams

UP NEXT: *SPORTS ZONE SPECIAL REPORT*

CREATORS

Scott Ciencin › Author

Scott Ciencin is a *New York Times* bestselling author of children's and adult fiction. He has written comic books, trading cards, video games, television shows, as well as many non-fiction projects. He lives in Sarasota, Florida with his beloved wife, Denise, and his best buddy, Bear, a golden retriever. He loves writing books for Stone Arch, and is working hard on many more that are still to come.

Gerardo Sandoval › Illustrator

Gerardo Sandoval is a professional comic book illustrator from Mexico. He has worked on many well-known comics including Tomb Raider books from Top Cow Production. He has also worked on designs for posters and card sets.

Benny Fuentes › Colorist

Benny Fuentes lives in Villahermosa, Tabasco in Mexico, where the temperature is just as hot as the sauce is. He studied graphic design in college, but now he works as a full-time colorist in the comic book and graphic novel industry for companies like Marvel, DC Comics, and Top Cow Productions. He shares his home with two crazy cats, Chelo and Kitty, who act like they own the place.

SPORTS ZONE
SPECIAL REPORT

BBL
BASKETBALL

PNT
PAINTBALL

FBL
FOOTBALL

BSL
BASEBALL

BBL
BASKETBALL

WINNING CHARACTER STANDS OUT FROM HUNDREDS OF ENTRIES IN NATIONWIDE STUDENT CONTEST!!

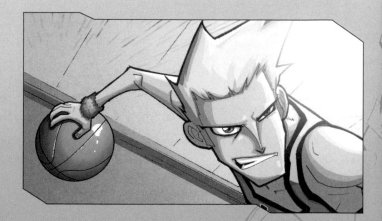

DASH THE FLASH

created by Justin Cox

Timmerman Elementary School
Pflugerville, Texas

Justin provided Stone Arch Books with a detailed description of his character. The level of thought and effort that Justin put into Dash the Flash's biography made it easy for our illustrators to bring this colorful character to life!

Sports Illustrated KIDS

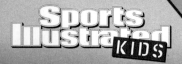

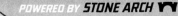

BLZ vs BHS
3-1
TGR vs ROR
33-32
EAG vs BAN
14-7
SPA vs WLD
4-3
BAN vs ROR
21-15
RZR vs LIG
4-3
BLZ vs BHS
3-1

Original design by
Gerardo Sandoval
and Benny Fuentes

Here's a few of the highlights from Justin's winning entry...

Character Name: Dash the Flash

Character Gender: Male

Physical Description: Suntanned, white, 6'6" tall, 212 lbs. Size 14 men's athletic shoes. Hands so large he can palm a basketball easily. His arms are so long that he has an unusually long wingspan.

Best Skill: He has outstanding peripheral vision

Worst Skill: Passing the ball — he gets too excited

Three words to describe him: Energetic, smart, skilled

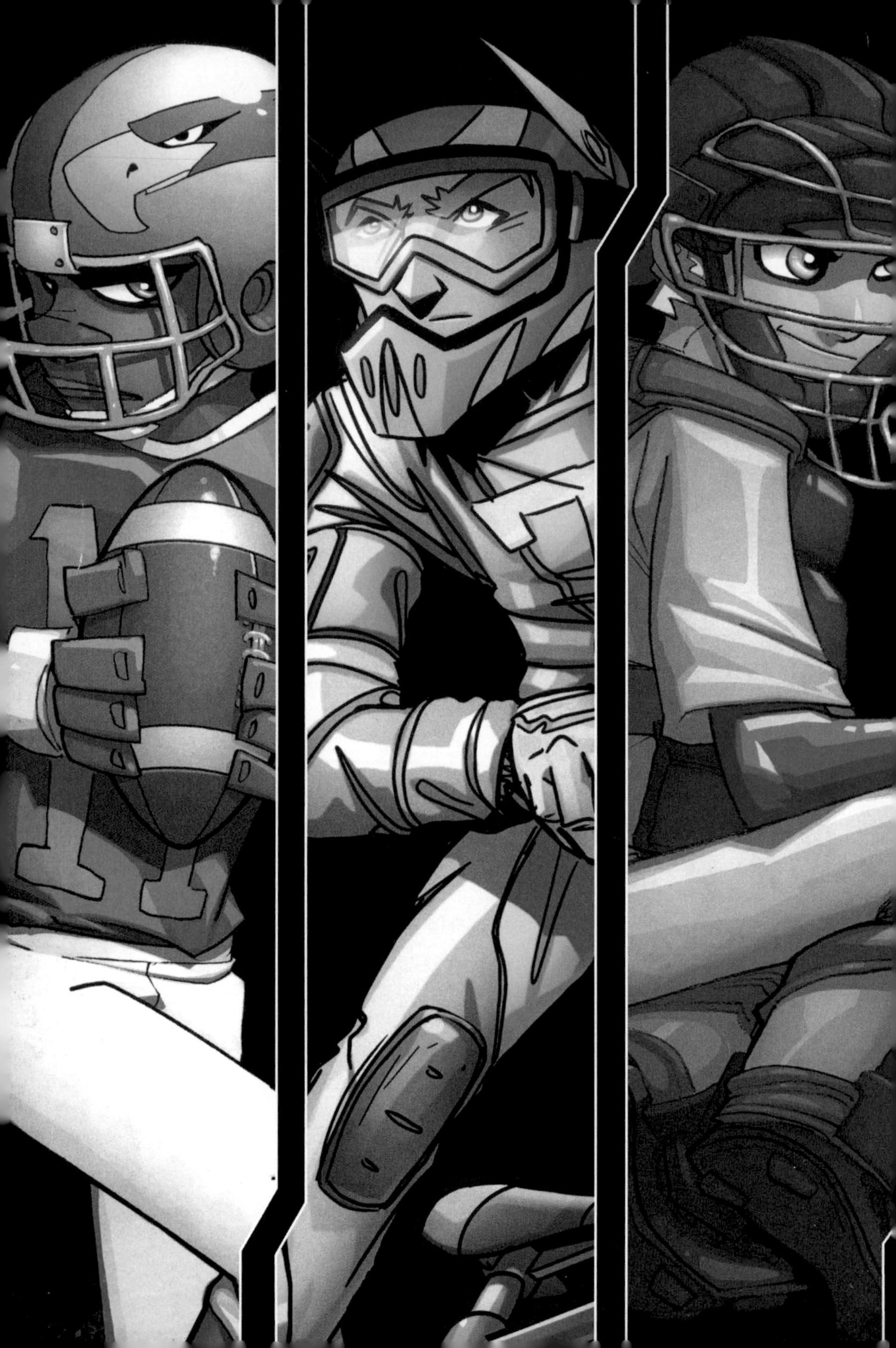

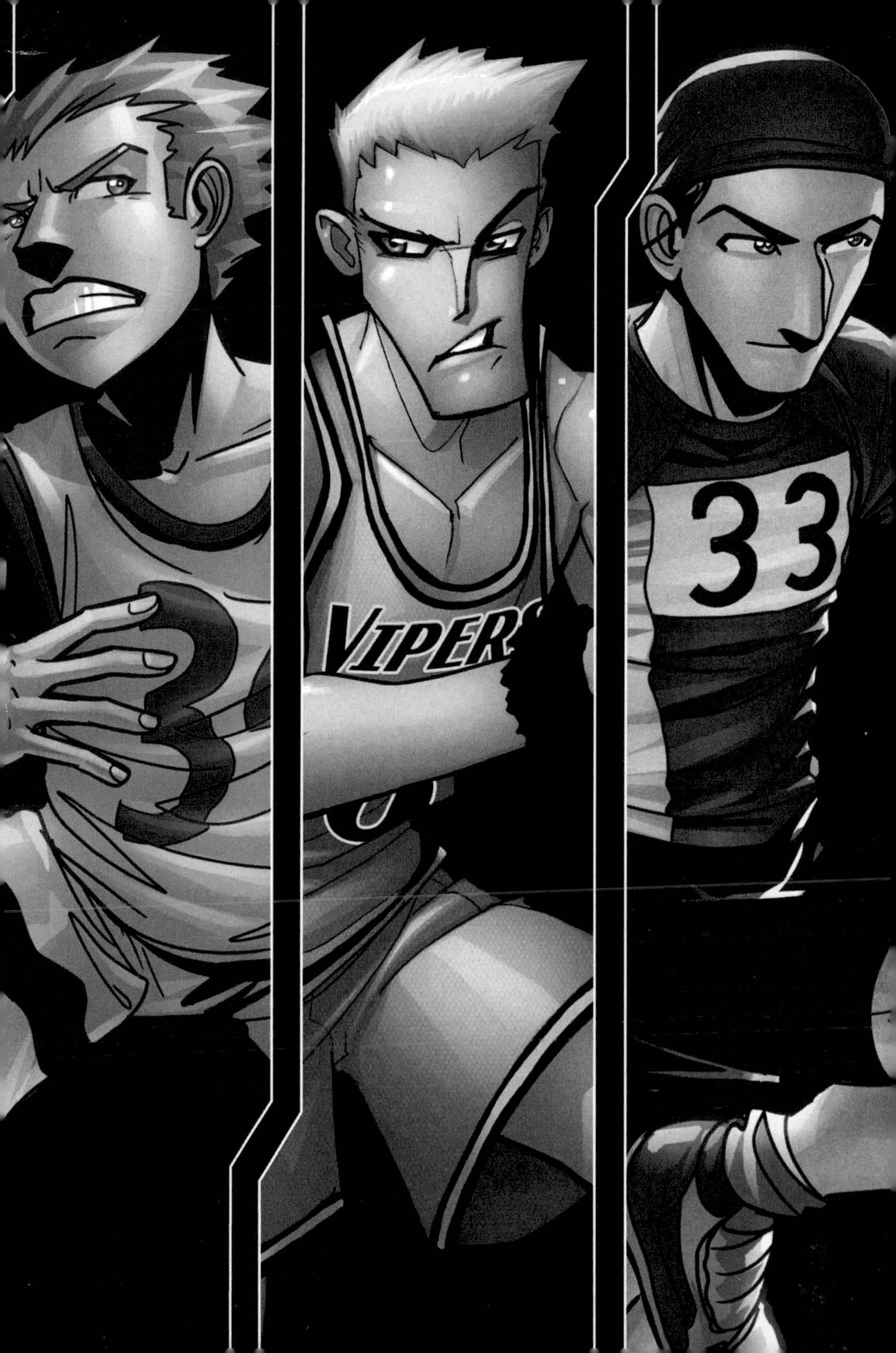
VIPERS
33

Sports Illustrated KIDS

GRAPHIC NOVELS

STONE ARCH BOOKS
a capstone imprint